A Love Like Ours Is Touching My Heart

The Love of My Life

Tony Glez

Table of Contents

Chapter 1:

Abigail

The city smog overwhelmed my lungs as I emerged from the subway station. Suitcase in tow, I dragged it across the expansive concrete, speckled with cracks and weather stains that denoted the age of the street. The soles of historians, celebrities, lovers, and generations of children had all walked these roads, their eyes gazing up at the brick buildings with their decadently etched gargoyles and entrances marked by expensive chandeliers. I caught myself wondering about the people around me—their voices surrounded me like a chorus, their lives, and predicaments the soundtrack to my arrival. Back home, I didn't have to think too hard about other people. They were few and far between, their personal bubbles unmarred by my presence. The closest I got to my neighbors was the long walk across our yard that opened up to a cornfield—which we rented out for extra cash—and in the distance, the tops of evergreen trees were visible along the horizon, dotted with the rooftops of my two or three companions. I had taken for granted those mornings sitting on Momma's porch, sipping coffee from a broken mug and watching the sun creep along the barren sky until it hung over us with its gentle heat. Now, I couldn't see anything other than buildings and plumes of gasoline.

I nudged shoulders and ran over toes as I attempted to navigate the streets of New York. I had heard rumors that it was the easiest place in the world to travel—all you had to do was follow the numbers on the lampposts and do a little math, and *boom*, you'd get where you were going. Apparently, the country roads I was used to were complex canals of never-ending stretches of pavement that only drew you deeper into the rolling hills and forests of Virginia. You could take a different route to the same location without even knowing it and without being able to retrace your steps the next time you needed to be there. But in New York? There was pretty much only one street you required and only one way to find yourself there. I didn't believe that to be true—not when I heard it the first time, and certainly not then as I stumbled into angry people yapping away on their cellphones, dusting off my touch as if I were nothing more than a pesky mosquito.

I contemplated asking for help, but I knew the venture would be useless. To them, I was a boneheaded tourist who deserved to be mugged for my stupidity—*that* would show me for being so foolish as to think I could survive this city—and not a girl who had recently lost her father. I didn't want to be in New York. I wasn't one of those angsty teenagers dreaming of discovering places bigger and better than my small town. I was content with my friends, all of whom I'd known since the first grade, and made decent money working as a waitress at a diner by the military base. Soldiers, especially the lonely ones, always tipped well, and my boss was like a dad to me. A real one. He wasn't the guy who took off on Momma when I was still a kid. He wasn't the one who opened up this damned bar that I was trekking out to, hoping to sell it for parts and use that to fund Momma's recovery. Why he couldn't have sent us money while he was still here was another one of his mysteries—I had to work to keep Momma alive, as I'd been working all my life to make up for the hole he left in our home. In our family. He got to leave breadcrumbs for me to follow, forever indebted to hearing the answers promised to me at the end of the rainbow.

My knuckles went white around my suitcase handle, and I knew I had to calm down. I was spinning out, holding my phone up to my ear as if I'd received a sacred call from some Good Samaritan who took pity on me. How they'd know about my tragedy would remain a divine secret, and I was fine with that. Anything to get me out of this hellhole, and quickly, wasn't going to be questioned. He couldn't have left me a map? If he wanted to go ahead and write me into his will, demanding, as part of his last wishes, that I oversaw his pride and joy, he could have at least assisted me in finding it. He was the one who pressed upon me the importance of land navigation—some of the lingering memories I had of him involved traversing the forest, compass in hand, pointing at rocks and tree stumps—making markings of our comings and goings. He showed me how to read the sunlight, feel the earth, and ask it questions. Most importantly, he taught me how to find home. Sometimes, I think he left us because he'd forgotten how to do that.

The other part of me wished it had been for a woman. Someone younger—a cliché, of course—without children or fine lines. Without obligations or predictability. Perhaps he had fallen victim to the listlessness of a quiet life, seeking adventure with a girl in her twenties who'd certainly break his heart. He bought the bar on a whim as an excuse to stay in the city she'd dragged him to, using the last of his savings to build some kind of monument to his flailing legacy. Now, he wouldn't have a child to carry on his name. He wouldn't have Momma's farm to coast off of, branding his lineage onto cardboard cartons of produce. So he had to come up with something, and a bar had all the trappings of a midlife crisis: booze, women, and drama. I rolled my eyes at the thought of him puffing up his chest to unruly patrons, showing men who looked up too many skirts the door, and feeling like a God as the women clamored to thank him for his act of chivalry. That certainly beat raising his daughter and taking care of his wife. Men who coveted their families were chumps.

I felt a rush of sickness as the tears flowed to my eyes. I despised thinking about him, or anyone, that way. I was tired of being bitter, of harvesting a resentment that only seemed to grow with age. I should have been over it by now—I was closer to 30 than my teenage years, yet I still felt as though my world was ending whenever I thought of him. I was mature enough now to know that life didn't operate in such extremes, that people would come and go, and usually, their faces would fade into vague shapes in my memory. And although I couldn't tell you much about him—what he looked like, what his favorite foods were, what he wore to bed—I still carried him around with me. Regretfully, he was tucked away in the pocket of my jeans, weighing me down like lead—banal, shapeless, and burdensome. I wished I could let go.

When I got the call, it was from the hospital. A surly doctor who failed to tell me his name demanded that I identify my father over the phone. He practically begged me to acknowledge the name. "Please, I have other patients," he hissed, "is Gerard Belmont your father or not?"

"Yes," I conceded weakly. I used that same small voice when his lawyer contacted me a week later.

It was heart failure—nothing violent or out of the ordinary. He was drinking and smoking, getting up there in years but trying to pretend he still had the body of a much younger man. He just wasn't taking care of himself, but who knows, he could have ended up in that hospital bed had he still been with Momma and me. There was no evidence to suggest he succumbed to an awful fate because of his transgressions. Momma didn't want me to frame it that way, either. She shed her tears silently as I relayed the news, one hand folded around my wrist and the other clutching the neckline of her sweater.

"I'm not his emergency contact?" she asked, her cheeks wet with grief.

I shrugged. "Guess not."

She crumpled into her rocking chair, trying hard not to look at me. "I was okay with the divorce, but... that's a little much, even for me."

We laughed about it. I wasn't sure why. Did she think that of all their broken vows, in sickness and in health would be the one he'd keep? I told him about Momma's illness when it got bad. Sure, I waited a while—could have said something sooner, and that's a mistake I'll have to atone for—but he didn't come back to check on her. Didn't ring her up one day just to ask how she was doing. He was sorry, and that was all. That was how I felt about his death, too. Sorry.

"What a shame," I caught myself telling both the doctor and lawyer. "He will be missed."

Sometimes, I worried my reaction was too demure for such an occasion. I feared the sound of knuckles rapping against our door, demanding answers for Gerard Belmont's sudden and untimely death. "Murdered by his own daughter," they'd say once they finally broke through the threshold. "Kids these days are so ungrateful."

One night, I found myself confessing my anxieties to Momma, and she gleefully rocked back and forth as she listened to my ridiculous tale. "If anything," she decried, "they'd come looking for me. A wife has more cause to kill her husband than his own kin."

"Are you really angry with him, Momma?"

"No," she said with a sigh, "of course not."

"You should be—"

"Well, I'm not, Abigail. And you shouldn't be, either. Life's too short for hurt feelings."

So there I was on the plane, chewing my gum like a lunatic, having never been in the air before. I didn't know what would happen when my ears allegedly popped. I didn't know what the sensation was like. I kept my jaw moving and my fingers roaming around my palms, gently digging my nails into my flesh whenever I had an unsavory thought. I had to go it alone—Momma was too sick to be moved, and my friends were tied up with their own lives. Most of them had kids and husbands, people who were waiting for them every night and waking up with them in the mornings. Sometimes, I watched them dote on their families and felt a lack, but I chalked it up to my loneliness. I just hadn't found the right man and didn't have the energy to wade through the admittedly slim pickings of the countryside. My friends tried to pump me up with fantasies of finding big love in the big city—I laughed them off and chided them for still harboring such childish imaginations. I swallowed the idea of romance, but perhaps sex was still on the table. I could stand to be touched, to be seen naked by a man who liked me enough for the night. The aches I felt coursing through my body were enough to send me into a tailspin—I needed to be satisfied, and my lonesome nights under the sheets couldn't keep me at bay for much longer. But nobody was out there for me, and even if they were, I wasn't ready to be let down again.

That's what I told myself as I finally spotted Dad's bar. The name was etched onto a plywood board, illuminated only by a few incandescent bulbs. The windows were shuttered with gaudy violet curtains, and the garbage bins outside the establishment were overflowing. People wouldn't miss a place like this—it was likely a bigger eyesore to the community than a treasure. I was doing them a favor by selling it. My Momma would heal, and so would the block. I'd finally be able to put the past behind me and leave my dad on the curb with the rest of the discarded junk.

Finally able to pull my phone away from my ear, I moved to shove it back in my pocket when—

"Hey!" I hollered instinctively. I tried to pursue the man in the army green jacket, but my suitcase was getting caught, the wheels toppling over with every crack they ran over. He rounded a corner, and then he was gone. Vanished with my phone.

"Help?!" I shouted to the onlookers as I gesticulated wildly, my words failing me when I needed them the most. Everyone turned their noses up at me. I was alone, left to fend for myself. "Fuck."

Chapter 2:

Paolo

"Letting me go... that's ridiculous."

"It's not *ridiculous*, Paolo, it's reality."

My boss—well, *former* boss—dabbed his sweaty forehead with a handkerchief as he shuffled a pile of meaningless papers on his lap. When he signed me to his label, I had made him promise to treat me like an artist, not a bottom line. Guess it was my fault for believing corporate scum had the capacity to appreciate music for the feelings it evoked, not the revenue it drew. Even then, my numbers weren't terrible; I had crowds waiting for me outside of venues and daily messages asking where my next album was. I thought this meeting was going to result in me finally getting answers to those questions, as I'd been hounding him for months to let me in a recording studio. Another mistake I made: relying on said corporate scum to get my work made.

"I'm not some pencil-pushing employee, Sal. I'm a *musician*."

"Big deal, kid. So's everyone else here."

"You? You're an artist?"

Sal glared at me from underneath his wired frames, his countenance sagging as his skin struggled to cling to his skull. I'd been fond of him—he seemed to appreciate my whims, allowing me to dictate the art direction of my photoshoots and music videos and entertaining my refusal to perform in shopping malls. I would have rather been penniless than caught dead in a Macy's peddling my tunes to a hoard of bored grandmothers looking for a new set of cheeks to pinch. That certainly wasn't going to help my image. If my desires were too costly or irritating, he shouldn't have let me carry on for so long. Just because

I had a vision didn't mean I was willing to sacrifice my entire career for it. I wasn't against selling out just a little bit. Or at least, reining myself in long enough to get the CEOs and suits off my case.

"You're just not charting, Paolo. I don't know what else to tell you."

"Who cares about charts?"

"We do. This is a business, not a charity."

"I can't chart if you don't give me the time to actually promote myself, you know? Play at notable venues, and—"

"It's been two years since your last album. You're not about to start selling out the Madison Square Garden."

"That's not what I'm saying. I don't even want that. I'm an underground artist writing and singing for the folksy types who actually appreciate and respect music."

Sal sighed. His frustration was palpable, and I soon came to understand that nothing I could say would change his mind. I had been axed, and unless I earned them a billion dollars overnight, there was no future for me with the label. "Give me a break, son. You're not saving the industry with your acoustic guitar and overgrown hair. It's time to let go."

"You used to be so nice, Sal." It came out almost like a whine, and for a moment, I was ashamed of my performance. I was too old to be grovelling.

"Back when you had potential, sure. But now? You're just a drain on our resources."

"We have a contract!" The anger rushed me all at once, and I stood from the plush leather armchair with a fury I didn't know I was capable of. No way they were going to turn me out on my ass just because I wasn't generating silly pop songs that teenagers could record themselves dancing to. I had integrity; I had a unique perspective—

"Learn to read the fine print."

And I was royally fucked. I sunk back into my seat. "I need the money, Sal."

"I'm not your bookkeeper. Or your accountant. Or your financier."

"I mean, you kind of are."

"Not. Any. More. Please, Paolo. It's time to go."

I wished I could have evacuated his office with a sworn promise to make him regret his decision. I wish I had left with my head held high, my ego unbruised, and bright opportunities still ahead of me. But I was a 27-year-old with hardly any savings, no lease to my name, and now no dreams to speak of. My parents had been riding my ass for years to finally wake up from my illusions, to be an adult and truly go to work. When I landed that deal and put my album out in record time, they finally backed off. That only lasted a few months—I still hadn't moved out of their place, and my schedule never seemed to rack up with gigs and meetings, signings, or parties. Sal was right about one thing: My debut had fallen into obscurity, and the only people ravenous for more were the groupies I'd managed to accumulate during my time as a singer at dive bars. That was my quote, unquote, day job before I had been recognized as a bona fide artist. That was the life I would be returning to; my head swung low as I pleaded with the owners of my old stomping grounds to give me another chance.

For all my bullshit, I hated being a disappointment. I was determined to make a living doing something honorable, sure, but I had chosen a difficult and often fruitless path to go down. I'd hoped my parents would find the plight somewhat noble, but the older I got, the less my pursuit was endearing. I'd dropped out of college for this, promising my parents that if I could just take advantage of those integral years in my youth, I'd be a rockstar in no time. If I was going to grind my way to the top, I had to be fuelled by hormones and adrenaline and quickly repair muscles the way only a teenage boy could. To be honest, I spent most of my days drinking in secret and hanging out at the park with people my mother would have deemed *vagrants*, using their stories to inspire my poetry, for they had lived and I had not. It was easier to siphon their misery, their rejection, their hustle than it was to generate my own. If anything, college would have given me something to write about, but I'd realized too late that I had doomed myself to roaming the streets, begging people to give me something to talk about.

It was Sal's fault, really, my fledgling album sales. He allowed me to use those hollow lyrics, laying them over guitar riffs that provoked an emotional reaction, further highlighting how hackneyed my writing had been. Why hadn't he stopped me? Had I really looked like dollar signs to him? I wanted to accuse him of steering me in the wrong direction, of tanking my career before it even got off the ground, but I knew it would accomplish nothing. So I dusted myself off and wordlessly exited the building, hopping on the first subway that would take me to Belmont's.

***

It was just after four o'clock when I took my place on the small beer-stained stage. Even the locals hadn't arrived yet, but I felt that if I began my set early, by the time I was hitting my peak, a crowd would be gathered around my feet. I could lure passersby in with my loud microphone dominating the air. Nobody was here to tell me to keep it down—George's death had left a vacancy in management they had yet to fill, and though I hated taking advantage of his absence, I knew that he would have understood my reasoning. He had always been my biggest supporter and often let me hop on stage between his paid acts' sets. I was never sure why he liked me so much—he didn't seem to absorb my music—but I wasn't about to question his unrelenting generosity.

Now, with my guitar tuned and my microphone brimming with life, I had command of the bar. I was going to make a name for myself, whether Sal or my parents wanted me to. I was tired of being doubted. Obviously, if I had been signed once, I had the talent to secure funding and management again. Though my previous label had lost faith in me, perhaps they weren't the right fit for my vision. If people shopped around for the perfect job in other careers, why wasn't I allowed to do the same? People expected me to lap up any praise I received as if I needed to be grateful for any and all opportunities, regardless of their merits. Perhaps Sal had dumped me because I had changed. After all, I was developing my sound and improving my skills. He didn't want or need an artist who was autonomous and didn't stagnate. He wanted predictable, reliable, and easy to push around. Those had never been traits I acquired.

The first strum reverberated through the near-empty bar with a fresh, luscious pulse. I had forgotten how exhilarating performing could be, for my concerts had grown few and far between. If I couldn't play dive bars at the behest of my management and refused to become a shopping center staple, it seemed I was relegated to local music festivals and the occasional opening act. It was bizarre to me. How long it took to open my eyes for me to wake up to the truth: I had been held down by the very contract I wanted to maintain. No wonder I had felt listless and deprived. I was stuck in my parents' house, waiting for something to happen while the promise of success loomed over my head. It was never going to come—not under Sal's watch.

My fingers ached as I continued to press on my guitar strings, sliding the pads of my fingers along the neck with an agility I didn't know I had. As I suspected, the place slowly started to fill out. The workday was over, and curious patrons trickled in, watching me with their arms folded as they waited for their pint of beer. Some had taken to sitting by the stage, crossing their legs as they attempted to hide their mild amusement, but I'd eventually win the showdown.

Some songs I concocted on the spot, allowing my mind to grow aflame with inspiration as I regarded the beautiful women who inhabited this city. I'd always wondered if the true void in my music was my inability to create a genuine love song. It wasn't that women were a market I was dying to exploit or that I wanted to diversify my repertoire— hitting on all the big emotions and lifetime achievements just to secure a fanbase—but that even I noticed a lack of heart in my discography. It was one thing to comment on the appearance of a woman, to compare her face to the natural wonders of the world, and another to actually mean it. Those who had never experienced love often failed to enunciate the delicacy of it. I knew my depictions weren't nuanced— they teemed with the obviousness of a man who struggled to form connections with other people. I inadvertently showed myself to be a player, lying his way into the bedrooms of multiple women, and that wasn't the image I wanted to project. I didn't like that version of myself, no matter how earnest it was. It just hadn't happened to me. Maybe I was to blame for my standoffishness, or maybe I was yet another victim of an increasingly hostile world. I didn't know. But I felt things starting to change when she walked in.

Her hair was tied messily to the back of her head, the strawberry blond strands cascading down her shoulders and across her face in frazzled, adorable wisps. Her cheeks were rosy, even in the dimness of the bar. A spotlight wasn't necessary to catch her pink glow. Her doe eyes stuck to me, their round, attentive gaze burrowing a hole in my skull. It was like she reached across the stage and tethered herself to me, telling me her name while her lips stayed slightly apart. I could write whole albums about her. And maybe I will.

Chapter 3:

Abigail

"Don't you guys have a phone back there?" I pleaded with the bartender. I assumed somebody would help me at Belmont's, especially when I told them who I was. My father had died only a week ago, and here they were, pretending as if I were a nuisance. As if my arrival was inappropriate. Was it really strange for the bereaved daughter of the owner to turn up after his passing? Maybe my father had opened his mouth one too many times, complaining about his unloving child. He set the groundwork for a hostile acquisition, prepping them for the day when I tried to burn what he had built to the ground. It was so typical of him to assume the worst of me, and I continued to pay the price of his distrust. Now, his loyal workers regarded me as a threat, unbelieving of my stories and my supposed loss. I guess they would be right about one thing: I did not miss my father. But my feelings weren't for them to determine, and especially not to use against me as I struggled in vain to get help.

The music had shortly stopped after I arrived, which was an unwelcome shift in the atmosphere. It was like I descended upon the building with a black cloud, casting anger and sadness over the staff without having to say a word. The man on stage practically rushed off once he spotted me; I was a pariah already. It was a shame, too, since the man had such a lovely voice. Maybe I wouldn't have been so irate had he kept going, his elegant words sedating me as I bargained with the bartenders. Maybe my issues would have been resolved already.

"Look," said the surly man behind the counter. His hair had been greased into spikes on the top of his head—he looked as though he walked out of an early 2000s music video. He wore an ironic bowling shirt labeled with a name that clearly wasn't his own, and his beard grew in uneven patches. "I can give you a beer on the house."

I rolled my eyes. "This *is* my house." He sloppily poured me something from the tap and placed it before me, liquid sloshing everywhere. "Thanks," I said dryly. I had always known New Yorkers to be rude, but I had expected at least a little sympathy from my father's establishment. I sipped the beer obligingly, understanding that maybe a drink would take the edge off. Just enough for me to flag down a willing stranger, that was.

"Hey," a voice said as the barstool scraped against the sticky floors beside me. Perhaps I wouldn't need to beg my case to every patron. When I turned to look at my savior, though, my heart fluttered. He had tousled, curly hair and a boyish grin that lit up his otherwise masculine features. His jaw was square and strong, his eyes small yet bright. He wore a plain, beige shirt that took a backseat as the rest of his countenance was amplified by the simplicity of his clothes. A dimple rested in the middle of his shapely chin.

"Hi," I replied weakly, "I liked your set."

"Really?" he asked, his tone somewhat sarcastic. His cadence was as lovely as his singing voice. "You only caught the last song."

"I'm always late to the party."

"That makes you sound like a true New Yorker, but judging by your luggage, I'd say you just got here."

I glared begrudgingly at my suitcase, hardly tucked under the bar. People bitterly stared at me as they attempted to avoid its bulk. "I never claimed to be from here," I retorted smoothly.

"No, I guess you're right."

"Judging by your smugness, I'd have to assume you're a native."

"Correct, again." He flagged down the bartender, who beamed generously at him. "Johnny—"

"Anything for you, Paolo," the man said, cutting my new companion off.

"You're the best," he replied with a wink.

"You seem to be a fan favorite around here," I began, "maybe you can help me."

"Not without a name."

"Abigail."

"Abigail?" He stuck out his hand, aiming to shake mine. The gesture was endearingly cordial; I had no choice but to accept his grasp. My hair stood on end as our skin touched, the warmth from his palm radiating through my arm and into my belly. "Paolo," he offered.

"Paolo," I repeated.

"What is it that you need, Abigail?" He leaned over the counter, his arms pressing into the wood until his muscles came into view under his sleeves. I found myself blushing at the sight, trying my best to avert my eyes as I debased myself before him.

"I just want them to let me use their phone."

"You don't have one?" he said with a laugh as if I was preposterously behind the times.

I hesitated. "I got mugged," I admitted in a small voice.

He forced down a smile. "This city can be so predictable sometimes."

"My fault for coming here."

"Come on," he said as he thrust his arms out, reaching them up to the sky in an exuberant display of pride. "This is the best city in the world."

"My stolen phone would have to disagree."

"You can just use mine." He dug it out of his pocket and handed it to me without another question. For some reason, the lack of transaction made me wary of his kindness. Why *hadn't* he behaved the way the others had? I was an outsider, hopelessly lost, and about to be a bigger drain on his time than he realized, and yet he interacted with me as if we were friends. "The guys 'round here can be meanies sometimes."

"You'd think I pissed in their sink with the way they've been treating me." Johnny, who overheard my comment, shot me a crippling look. I winced as I accepted Paolo's phone.

"Who're you calling, anyway? If you don't mind me asking."

I bit my lip, realizing I didn't have the answer to that question. What did I plan on doing? If I told him I needed help finding my phone, maybe he would entertain tracking it down with me. I could bank on his niceness for a little while longer, enough to retrieve my things, anyway. Then again, the more I needed from him, the more he could wind up feeling owed something. "Hotels, I guess."

"Which one?"

I shrugged.

"Oh no." He ripped the phone from my hands. "No, no, no."

"What?" I was amusingly shocked.

"You can't go looking for a hotel without a plan. You're gonna get ripped off!"

"I may have just been robbed, but I'm not *that* dumb."

"Abigail, this is the most expensive place to be for a tourist—"

"—probably not the *most* expensive."

"You're better off staying with me for the night."

I scoffed, my jaw growing slack. Though, admittedly, I didn't hate the proposition.

"Not like that," he corrected himself. "My parents have a spare room you can stay in. You'll have Wi-Fi, an old computer for you to use, and a private bathroom. Save your money for the new phone you're gonna have to buy."

I feigned mulling it over, fearing I was making myself into an easy target by being so willing to accept his generosity. "That would be nice, but..."

"But?"

"I feel like this is a no-no. Stranger danger and all." I blushed at my own proclamation. It was childish.

He smirked as he took a swig of his beer. "I hate to say it, but you're a bit old for that, aren't you?"

"Haven't you heard?" I giggled, finally starting to feel the effects of the alcohol. "Twenty-six is the new sixteen."

He pursed his lips as he looked away. "Gross." Had I taken it too far? I wasn't used to flirting. Was that what I was doing? Usually, boys just announced they were taking me out and oftentimes decided they were my partner without my having a say in the matter. I'd thought I liked that system—it took all the guesswork and buildup out of the equation—until now, sitting beside a man I wanted. Or could want. I shouldn't get ahead of myself. "Now I feel like a perv."

"Why?" I asked, attempting to sound coy. Attempting to recuperate from my misstep.

He shook his head. "Just tell me what you're doing here, eh? Small fish in a big city."

"Oof." It was my turn to drink. "Dark subject."

"Really?"

"My dad died." Why did I lead with that? I watched his brows furrow as he struggled to decide whether to console or chide me for such a personal remark. I blundered on anyway—if I lost him, that fate had already been sealed. "This is his bar. He left it to me, but... I can't take care of it."

"Nonsense!" he decried, his energy returning. "The place practically runs itself: a well-oiled machine. Isn't that right, Johnny?" The bartender slid him another pint, a smile plastered on his face.

"I don't know. I think selling it will get me the money I need. And a lot faster, too."

Paolo's expression grew cold. He inched away in his stool as if he no longer wanted to be near me. "Money... that's all you people think about." He shook his head, bowing over the counter as if to close off our conversation.

"Um, I'm sorry," I said awkwardly. My tone clearly indicated that I didn't mean it. "But... my dad *died*. What do you want me to do? Shackle myself to this place for the rest of my life? For a man who didn't give enough of a... you know what? I'm not doing this." I started gathering my things, chugging the remains of my beer as I got up to leave. I stuck his phone into the periphery of his vision, but he refused to acknowledge it.

"This place means a lot to people," he muttered, still avoiding my gaze. "Including me. *Especially* me. It... it inspires practically all of my music."

"I don't know you, man. I can't live my life in servitude to your music."

"People think they can just walk into this city and change shit. They wanna tear down buildings and put up glass towers. They wanna evict the small businesses for the big shots. They don't respect the history or the culture or all the people who proudly walk around telling everybody about their beautiful home. I love being from New York. I'm proud of this place. I can't take any more destruction."

I stared at him incredulously, unsure of how I got roped into the realtors and millionaires who were gutting establishments for a quick profit. "Listen, Paolo, I get it. Fuck gentrification and all that, but this is nothing personal."

"Oh, to you, maybe it's not—"

"My mom's dying."

"Great sob story."

Now, my blood was boiling. Who did this guy think he was? Was he the mayor of New York? Did he get to boss me around and dictate how others lived their lives because his interests came above all else? The arrogance that exuded from him for simply having a fine singing voice was astounding. "The world doesn't revolve around you, Paolo. I'd rather save my mom than this stupid bar just so you have somewhere to play. Maybe get some real talent, and people will wanna hire you."

"It's not that simple."

"But owning and running a bar is?"

"It could be!"

"Get real, Paolo! What fucking fantasy do you live in? Are mommy and daddy funding your pathetic career, and that's why you can waste your time playing at some dump to an audience of one? There are no stakes to that! Try paying some bills, and maybe then you'll get it." I shook the phone in his face, desperately trying to force him to turn around. To look at me. "Will you just take your goddamn phone back?"

He held his position with a bizarre stoicism and spoke in a low, stern voice: "Not until you promise to keep Belmont's, Abigail."

Chapter 4:

Paolo

"Alright, that was a bit dramatic," I admitted, finally allowing my eyes to drift over to Abigail. Her cheeks had grown red, like ripe tomatoes, and her chest was rising and falling at a rapid pace. She was losing her mind just talking to me, and I didn't blame her. I had flown off the handle without a second thought, ready to accuse a stranger of ignorance and maliciousness because she was taking something away from me. Something that wasn't even mine. But without Belmont's, what was I supposed to do? The place had become my entire source of income over the last few years, and I couldn't let that slip through my fingers. Not without enough warning to actually land on my feet. I had to bargain with this beautiful devil.

"You think?" she shot back, folding her arms across her chest, successfully hiding my phone behind her gorgeous mane.

Why did such an enchanting woman have to be in control of my fate? The lust I felt for her was driving my brain wild, coaxing me into experiencing all of my emotions at an intensity that was rather uncomfortable and certainly not helpful to my predicament. She was right: Her father had just died, a crappy bar had been dropped in her lap, and now here I was, scolding her for not reading my mind and preserving its history. I was tempted to drop my gaze from her angelic face, unsure that I could calm myself down if I continued to look at her.

"Can we strike a deal?" I offered.

"No," she hissed, "You don't get a say in what I do with my bar. Get it? *My bar.*"

"Look, I understand that you don't wanna be stuck here. You wanna go back to—" I faltered, realizing I hardly knew a thing about this woman.

"Virginia," she said.

"Right, Virginia." She really was a country mouse trying to navigate the chaos of New York. She almost endeared herself to me then, without trying. Just being herself. I caught myself in another whirlwind of emotions I struggled to keep at bay. I had no choice but to avert my eyes. "And you can. But you think a silly little sale is gonna settle that in just a few days?"

She frowned, "Well, I don't know, Paolo." I loved it when she said my name. "I don't know what the fuck I'm doing, can't you tell?" She waved my phone in my face, signalling her earlier blunder.

"Do you even have a buyer?"

It was her turn to look away. "No."

"So, what was your brilliant plan?"

"I don't—ugh, like, close up shop. Put it on the market. Let a broker handle the whole thing and have it off my hands in a few days. Doesn't life move fast around here? One day, this is Belmont's, and the next, it's a pizza joint. The pizza joint lasts a few years, and then it's something else."

I was awash in relief as she spoke. She was going to flounder in a few days, likely running out of money as the reality of her situation came crashing down on her. She didn't have the street smarts to hire a reliable broker and was certainly overestimating how hot the market was. She was getting all her intel from movies and TV shows, evidently, and if she was that strapped for cash, she wasn't going to survive in the city long enough to see her little plan come to fruition. She was toast; I had the advantage.

"I know you don't wanna trust me right now," I began, "but believe me when I say you're gonna need a lot more patience trying to sell this place. Shutting it down is just a drain on your future bank account.

Food will go rotten, rats will run amuck, and suddenly, the millions you could've had for the place will be mere pennies. Don't be stupid."

"I'm not stupid," she mumbled solemnly.

"I'm not saying that you're actually stupid, but I'm saying you need to do more research. Keep the place open and host buyers on a nightly basis. Ply 'em with drinks, show 'em the crowds, convince 'em what a great space this is. You'll have to do some schmoozing, but it's the right call. Do you want this bar gone?"

"Yes."

"Then will you agree to do as I tell you?" She opened her mouth to fire back, but I silenced her with my palm. "Like, keep the lights on until you've actually landed a deal, Abigail. That's all."

The fire in her expression diminished again. "Okay."

"Shake on it?" I extended my hand out to her once more. She stared at it warily. "If you're scared that this is bad business practice, don't be. I have no reason to screw you or Belmont's over. I already told you how much this place means to me."

She accepted my offer, sliding her skin against mine and squeezing my fingers. Electricity radiated through my nerve endings, sending signals throughout my body that couldn't be ignored. Not for long. "You know," she said, "I'm still going to stay in a hotel."

"Don't worry, you're uninvited, anyway."

The tension between us seemed to melt, and a coy smile crept back on her plump lips. I couldn't stay angry with her, either, feeling a magnetic pull toward her as she meekly ordered another beer. Despite our fight, she was staying. How odd. How magnificent.

"You were probably going to lie to your parents about me," Abigail blushed, "I bet they're desperate for you to get a girlfriend. Hell, at your age, you should have a few kids and a wife."

"That makes sense. The pervert husband, sick of his old bag, turns to a young girl for comfort."

"Ew," she replied with a laugh, playfully pushing me with her free hand. The other was still tightly wrapped around my phone.

"Can I have that back now?" I asked.

"This?" She pointed to it, a goofy expression on her perfect features. "I'm sorry, Sir, but you didn't hold up your end of the bargain."

"Keep it, keep it open; same thing."

"I'm afraid not."

"Come on."

"You don't get to make *all* the rules, Paolo."

"I certainly do. And you'll come to find that out shortly. But for right now, I can offer you a couple hundred bucks for a replacement phone."

"Are you buying me off?" she asked with a laugh.

"Honestly? No," I admitted. "I just can't stand sending a lady out into the city lost and defenseless."

"Paolo to the rescue." It was apparent now that the alcohol was starting to impact her. I'd have to give her a lift to a hotel, too, ensuring she was tucked away safely before I could fathom retreating to my own home for the night. I was confident she wouldn't mind. Not with the way she was staring at me, her eyes piercing my soul with their gentle, longing pressure.

"Exactly."

***

Unfortunately, the lights were on when I finally shuffled into the apartment. It was just past midnight, and I assumed my parents would be asleep. They always seemed to be curled up in bed these days, feigning weakness whenever I was home in an attempt to drive me insane. The only way they could convince me to leave their abode was if they bored me to tears. The charade made me laugh more than anything—it was playful at heart, and their intentions weren't to leave me out on the street with nothing to my name. They knew I had the capacity to lead a great life, but they felt I needed a push. I didn't see how living on my own would accomplish that. If anything, it would further my circle down the drain.

However, as I kicked my shoes off at the entryway, it slowly dawned on me how pathetic the arrangement had become. I was offering my bedroom to random girls who flirted with me at bars, pretending as though I was a chivalrous knight and not an adult still living like a kid. What would have happened had Abigail taken up my offer? She'd watch me pack up my bedding and transfer it to the couch, putting the puzzle pieces together as the alleged guest room—coincidentally decorated with all my achievements and interests—displaced me for the evening. She would have laughed herself out the door, shaming me for my predicament. She wanted to know who I thought I was, bossing her around? I was the loser without any prospects, trying to tell her how to manage her finances.

I hated dogging on myself, but as I approached my parents, sitting on their matching recliners in the living room with two steaming cups of tea on the coffee table, I had the sinking feeling that I was too old to still be joining them. Not on a nightly basis, that was.

"Where were you, Pinky?" Mom asked as she blew on her mug.

"I told you not to call me that," I muttered.

She shrugged, "Now you're too grown up..."

"Darling," my dad interjected, "he just got in. Let's not jump down his throat."

"Alright," she conceded, shooting me a look. Even in her attempt to be brutal, the kindness in her eyes betrayed her. I knew she loved me, even with all my supposed failures. I just needed a little more time than the other sons in the neighborhood, that was all. She'd understand that one day.

"I was at Belmont's," I said, taking a seat on the couch across from them.

"Typical," my father chortled.

"Some chick is trying to sell it."

"Don't use that language," my mom chastised me again.

"Is she selling it to you?" Dad asked.

"No. She doesn't care who buys it, just that they do."

"So?" came Mom. "What's the problem?"

I shifted in my seat. "The neighborhood—"

"Oh my God," she cut me off, "I've had enough of this. If it's not you, it's the building. If it's not the building, it's the baggers at the grocery store. Everybody's all worried about protecting these couple blocks, but you know what? You can't stop change. It's happening. The way we live now surely caused a stir with the people who were here before us. They didn't want us coming here with our big innovations and gas appliances."

"I don't think that's historically accurate."

"Jeez, Paolo. Your mother isn't a professor, okay? I'm just saying you can't keep fighting the inevitable."

"Like getting a wife," Dad offered.

"Exactly. Like getting a wife. Was this girl pretty?"

I rolled my eyes, the truth threatening to reveal itself on my features. My parents were always trying to pawn me off on every girl who walked within a 3-mile radius. If I performed at a bar, they asked me how many girls talked to me after the show. If they caught up with an old friend, they told me about all their single daughters. They were perpetually stuck in the '50s, ashamed that their poor boy had yet to settle down—he was running out of time. As much as their desperation pissed me off, it wasn't like I didn't echo their sentiments.

"Yeah, she was fine," I admitted.

"That means she's a knockout," my dad said with a laugh.

"Finally," my mother cheered, "we'll have him out of the house."

I shook my head and wordlessly stalked off to my room. It felt empty tonight—barren of warmth, affection, fulfillment. It would have been nice to tiptoe into a bedroom in an apartment I owned, where the love of my life was still half-awake in bed, waiting up for me in tepid worry. She knew I'd come home, that I was always safe, but still, her mind raced with the *what ifs*. I'd kiss her on the forehead and let the weight of my lips compel her to sleep. It was okay. Now, she could rest easy. I shuddered at my own fantasy, feeling as though I'd fallen into a trap of some sort. I couldn't rely on someone else to fix me. I couldn't roam around this earth, blaming my misery on all the women who refused to love me. That wasn't my style. I was fine. I'd continue to be fine. I just had to keep chugging along.

Chapter 5:

Abigail

I had a headache as I walked into the obnoxiously bright store. Nursing a coffee I had picked up at what the locals referred to as a *bodega*, I sauntered over to the counter where a male employee, doused in cologne, was eagerly greeting me with a smile. Despite my stay in a hotel, I felt as though I'd had the worst sleep of my life. The air conditioner was blasting all night, plugging my sinuses and sending unnatural shivers down my spine. The comforters may have been ample and pulled tight around the corners of the mattress, sealing me in, but the frigid temperature managed to creep in regardless. The shadows in my room shifted in size, taking on the shape of all the deceased residents of such a haunted city, and the honking on the streets below never ceased. Not even as the clocks knelled around four o'clock in the morning when not even the most dedicated worker was commuting to the office. Still, their horns blared.

I had a dream, too, between my waking hours. Paolo had come to me, his soft raps on the door wooing me into letting him in. He pinned me against the wall, making me taste his fingers as he slowly unbuttoned his jeans. He was gentle as he picked me up, laying me on the bed with ease. I swore the weight of his body moving along mine was real. I could feel the impressions of palms and his hard cock against my inner thighs. I bucked my hips to reach him, to feel the full extent of the pleasure he was offering me, but it never came. I quivered throughout the night, struggling to keep my mind off his sensuous body and coy smile. Struggling to keep myself satisfied.

I was carrying the cash Paolo had given to me, feeling dirty somehow for using it. We hadn't exactly gotten off on the right foot, and there was always a chance he was using that act of kindness as a bargaining chip. He'd spin it so that I owed him something down the line, like keeping the bar under my name indefinitely, so long as that served his purposes. I attempted to dissolve my thoughts of him—his sweet smile, his perfect hair, his magnetic body—as I rested my coffee on the counter and addressed the employee.

"I need a new phone," I proclaimed and proceeded to reject every option the worker laid out for me that involved too much navigation and setup. I needed something I could walk out the door with in working condition, without all the bells and whistles. I was a simple girl—what was I going to do with the highest tech in the countryside?

The employee was peeved by my insistence on purchasing a basic, but after 20 minutes of our terse row, he finally waved a white flag. As I handed him the cash, I noticed blue ink smudged along the backside of a bill. I snapped it up, much to the worker's dismay, and held it up close. It was, without a doubt, Paolo's number.

"Sorry," I murmured to the employee. I grabbed the phone, still in its packaging, off the countertop and inputted the contact information without a second thought.

***

I was in another bleakly lit office not too long after, staring quizzically at the contraption I had just bought and guzzling down my second cup of coffee. I wore sunglasses as if I were suffering from a hangover, my eyes sensitive to the ample fluorescent lights, and an oversized men's sweater. I hadn't thought about presentability as I rushed out the door to make it to the airport in time, but now that I was surrounded by fashion models and suits, I was well aware of my maladjusted appearance. There was nothing that I could do, though, as my luggage was overtly small in anticipation of a quick turnaround. I hoped Paolo was wrong and that I'd be on my way home shortly with the checks I required. I hoped my dowdy outfit wouldn't compel the lawyer, sitting before me in his cushy ergonomic chair, to disregard my father's final wishes and entrust his business to someone who actually mattered. Someone who was kempt, professional, and worthy. Someone even Paolo would approve of. Never had I felt so rejected by people and for reasons so banal that I couldn't decide whether to be offended or not.

"So..." he breathed, his eyes scanning a sheet of paper. He set it on the waxed oak desk once he'd found what he was looking for and enclosed his fingers together. He stared at me directly, his gaze as firm as a handshake. "Ms. Belmont?"

I clucked my tongue instinctively.

"No? You're not...?"

He was about to return to his pages when I interjected. "I mean, yes, I am. Mr. Belmont's daughter, that is. I guess I just haven't been that in a while."

"Semantics," he stated plainly, returning to his assured stance. "No place for that in legalese."

"Sorry," I blushed, feeling my inadequacy taking hold.

"It's my duty to your father to protect his estate," the lawyer continued, "and while I'm happy to hand over the deed and the keys to Belmont's, I'd also like to impart a few suggestions in terms of buyers, if that's alright."

"Of course. Any information helps. I don't—I don't really know what I'm doing..."

"I can tell." His expression didn't waver, and I couldn't read his eyes. Was he ashamed of me? Had my father really made such an impression on the people of New York that they were all sullen at my presence? I was Godzilla, a destroyer of cities, it seemed.

"Is selling a bad idea?" I asked quietly, my paranoia getting the better of me.

"No," he replied quickly and with a shake of his head. "It's smart, young lady. I help people conduct business, not feelings, and Belmont's is as unprofitable as they come. Sell the lot; you'll get more out of it that way. Your dad was on the brink of it, anyway."

"It's just... everybody's been telling me what to do, and none of that has been to sell, and—"

"And they don't know what they're talking about, either. I do. It's my job; talking, thinking, helping. Sorting through the bullshit. Besides, it's not written in his will that his daughter must, under any and all circumstances, maintain his bar. It's been entrusted to you with the intent of allowing you to do what you want. That is his gift, Ms. Belmont. It's not a punishment."

I stifled a laugh as the relief swathed over me. "Lately, it's been feeling that way."

"It's human nature, dear, to regard death as a punishment. I'd say it's a new opportunity."

***

I struggled to jam the keys into the front door as the buyer loomed behind me, a permanent grimace on her sharp face and a *tap-tap-tap* that emanated from her outdated ballet flats. Not only had the lawyer given me a few suggestions for real estate investors, but he also had the courtesy to arrange the first viewing for me. Unfortunately, he'd overestimated how prepared and capable I was to deal with such a matter and wound up in the same ratty clothes I'd visited him in, my fingers crinkling the deed as the other hand sloppily attempted to navigate the locking mechanism on the front door.

What awaited me on the other side of the threshold was also to be a mystery, as I clearly hadn't won any of the workers over, and I had no clue as to how the place was run. Did the buyer care about looks, or was she interested in the lot? Wait, that was a good question to ask her. I whirled around and shot her the most charming smile I could muster, even as the sight of her boney knees, thin lips, and crusty, blond hair wound in tight ringlets looked back at me. For all my fears about presentability, at least I had a face that made up for what I lacked.

"Do you plan on taking over the bar? Or are you just looking at the building? Like, it's structure and stuff."

"Shouldn't you *know* what I want?" she retorted.

I crumpled a bit as I returned to the pesky keys, finally hearing the glorious *click* of the gears shifting into place. Attempting to mask my joyous pride, I rubbed my hands over the walls until they located the light switch. Once the place was illuminated, she scurried in ahead of me and began picking apart the place with her harsh eyes. I nervously hung back, not wanting to be interrogated for the state Belmont's was left in.

Mop buckets were sprawled across the various floors—both on the black and white, checkered tiles in the performance hall and the authentic wood of the bar area. Scuff marks were engrained in both materials, but I didn't find the imperfections to be unsightly. No, I quite liked knowing people had been here. They had danced, fell down, spilled drinks, and fell in love. They made friends with my father and felt comfortable sitting on his cracked leather barstools. Took to Belmont's after work for the sake of routine and familiarity. People, including my dad, had lived their whole lives here, and their movements could be tracked in the gray scratches on the floor.

While the concert venue was blacked out, with a giant curtain hanging over the windows to prevent any bustle from the outside world streaming in, the bar was cozy and quaint. Stained glass windows littered the outskirts of the room, adorning every booth with fragmented colors. The seats themselves looked like church pews, and I wondered if my father had done that on purpose. He was never a religious man, but he had confessed to being envious of the Catholics—they had all that lore, all that history, and all those paintings. He'd longed to make something as impervious to time and criticism. Belmont's was evidently his chapel, but it hadn't protected him from the buyer's disdain.

She stalked over to me with her arms folded, and said, "Can I see the kitchen?"

I nodded. "Of course."

I led her behind the bar and through the double metal doors. Surely, she would be frightened by the scene before her—food had been left out on counters, sauce stains crusted to the walls, and a host of health code violations were present on every surface and appliance. Even I, who had never worked in a kitchen, understood that things weren't up to snuff. I could have run around attempting to hide the rotten rags and covertly clean the dishes, but it would have been a waste. For a moment, I understood what Paolo loved so deeply about Belmont's. Or perhaps I was finally experiencing the grief over my father's death I assumed would never come. Knowing he had built something, that he had hovered over the cooks and tasted their meals, that he had signed off on the furniture and the selection of beers, and that he had found himself pleased with his work made me resent him a little less. Why he couldn't have done this back in Virginia I'd never wrap my head around, and I didn't think I'd ever forgive him, but at least I was starting to see the man he had become. The man he never was for me. Was that really such a bad thing?

Though I was aptly aware that whatever meal I ordered later tonight would be a risk to my health, I wanted to stick around until opening. I wanted to try the food my father had packed up his whole life for. Would I be able to do that if the buyer put in an offer?

"So, what do you think of the place?" I asked, pulling myself out of my haze.

"It's grotesque," she replied brusquely, "but I'm not looking to revamp the place. It's basically a junkyard for parts, and then the bare bones will be fashioned into something much more... timeless. I'm thinking a series of condos."

"Oh," I mumbled, noting the way my heart dropped in my chest. Hadn't this been what I wanted? "But the neighborhood will get up in arms about the change. Aren't you worried about that?"

"Please," she chortled, "they'll be begging to live here, and then they won't be able to afford the cost."

"Isn't that cruel?"

"I'll offer you twenty percent over asking."

Just then, the air became aflame with the noise of crackling and static, followed by a man clearing his throat into an obnoxiously loud microphone. "Check, check—check one, check two." It was Paolo.

I stormed out of the kitchen, my emotions over the sale momentarily replaced by my anger for such a man, daring to enter my property and then attempting to dissolve my business.

"Hey!" I hollered, balling my hands into fists.

"Abigail!" he called back. "This one's for you."

Then Paolo proceeded to play the worst song I had ever heard.

Chapter 6:

Paolo

"I'm so sorry," Abigail cooed, her flute-like voice going up a few octaves as she fought to control her rage.

I sat triumphantly on the stage, the hum of my amps still ricocheting across the venue. I had purposely flubbed it, cracking my voice and pushing it out of my throat with a nasal twinge. If the buyer thought this place came with a handsome musician crooning over an acoustic guitar, she would have bought the bar in a heartbeat. I wasn't looking to help Abigail, even if that would have benefitted me in a whole other way. No, I wanted to sink her. I wanted to watch as she flailed her arms around, trying and failing to unplug my setup to put me on mute. It was adorable how hard she worked at it, seemingly perplexed by my basic assemblage of cords. She would have destroyed the bar had she taken over as owner or even just the middleman in a transaction, and that was something I had to factor into my plan. This wasn't just about saving Belmont's: Abigail had to be snipped out of the picture, too.

My heart twitched at the idea of her absence, and I found myself swallowing my elusive feelings as they cropped up like bile. There was no way I could mourn the loss of a woman I hardly knew, especially not when I was the one who planned on driving her out. My lack of conviction was going to burden me if I didn't get a handle on things.

"As you can see," continued Abigail, "I'm new here. I don't know this man." She gestured to me. "I don't know how to make him leave. I'll have to discuss that with the staff. I just got handed the deed, and all I want is for this property to go away. You can have it."

"I'm not sure," the snooty woman replied, looking at me up and down with malice. "I didn't get a good look."

"I thought you said—"

"And some new developments have cropped up."

"We can reschedule."

"Alright. Next Tuesday." She swung around on her polished heels and beelined for the door, her shoes *clacking* on the way out.

"Fuck you," Abigail spat at me once the daylight ceased to infiltrate this hallowed hall and we were alone.

Now, I was off the stage, rushing over to her side as if she were a wounded child. Did I mean to mock or comfort her? "I had to," I pleaded, a cloying grin spreading across my lips.

"I was literally doing what you told me to do!"

She fled as soon as I encroached on her space, my palm reaching for her enflamed cheek. She stormed into the bar, where Johnny had slipped in during the throes of my scene, and began quietly polishing glassware for the evening's business. When Abigail noticed him, she scowled, her nose scrunched up like she smelled something foul. Even with a pucker, her face was still radiant.

"Not really," I clarified.

"God, you are *such* a child." She began to pace around the floor, realizing she was trapped by two men who didn't have an ounce of sympathy for her. Or at least, that's what she assumed of us.

"Why don't you just calm down?" I knew the remark would irritate her, especially as I motioned for her to drop her levels with my hands. She nearly wrung my neck, her eyes ablaze with fury. The more I sparked her emotions, the giddier I felt. She harbored something for me— desire, passion, rage. Watching her countenance contort as she faced me was like a fireworks show.

"What did I ever do to you?" she shot back, finally jabbing me in the chest with the tip of her pointer finger.

"Sell Belmont's."

"You agreed that I should!" She was desperate, her chest heaving as she struggled to sync her breathing with her speech.

"And I was wrong."

"We shook on it!"

"So?"

"So?!" Exasperated, she crumpled into a booth, allowing her forehead to gently smack against the table. Johnny rushed over with a pitcher of beer and a stack of plastic cups, eyeing me as he swaggered back to his dish duty. "Why, Paolo?" she sobbed.

"Belmont's should be run by a Belmont," I replied, my brain suddenly singing a different tune. Did I really want her to be the owner, or was I buttering her up in hopes she'd seriously calm down?

"I can't run this place, and you know it."

"No, I don't," I lied.

"And I don't want to. That's what matters here: I don't want to." Authentic tears were welling in her doll-like eyes.

"But why not? If you learn the ropes, all you'll really need to do is come in a couple days a week and make sure everything's still running smoothly. That's what your pops did. Everybody here is trained, and business is good. You'll make easy money just letting everybody do their thing."

"Who made your brand ambassador? Are you even on the payroll?" She picked up a plastic cup and filled it up poorly, all the foam racing to the surface. She drank it anyway, and I joined her, amused by her roller coaster of emotions.

"You'll find out," I said, "if you choose to work here."

"I can go in the back right now and look at whatever paperwork I want, okay? But I'm not cut out for this."

"Then what are you meant to do?"

She shook her head, the tears finally rolling down her cheeks as the feelings she'd been clinging to gave way. Maybe I shouldn't have pushed her so hard. I was enthralled, yes, but I wasn't a sadist. "I don't know," she replied meekly.

"What's your job back home?" I asked, my tone easing up in an attempt to disarm her.

"I'm—I'm a waitress."

"Oh, come on."

"What?"

"You're perfect for this! What, with all the people pleasing, and the customer service, the food regulations... you'll have this place memorized and operational in no time." What I thought was kindness on my end wound up driving her further into her hysteria.

"I can't do this forever," she cried, "I thought I'd have a passion by now. A dream, I don't know. Something silly but simple."

"Hey, listen, following your dreams doesn't always pan out." I placed a hand on hers. "I mean, look at me. I'm almost thirty, Abigail, and I'm fighting for a bar I sometimes sing at to stay open. You know why? It's the only place that'll consistently put me on the books. I had a record deal before this."

"Really?" Her wet cheeks were drying, and she sped up the process with her free hand, wiping away the excess water.

"Mhm," I confirmed, "an album, too. I thought that meant I'd made it, and I'd be going on world tours, having people show me my name tattooed on their bodies, getting awards and stuff. Everything that I'd worked toward—skipping school, living in a shitty situation, earning next to nothing—I thought it'd been worth it. But I'm still here. Still at Belmont's."

"But you live in New York," she gently protested. "You should be able to make it here. There's always more time."

"That's the problem: People think that just by being here, things will happen. Growing up, I thought I was the luckiest kid in the world. I got to walk by studios where some of the greats recorded their albums every day. I knew that whenever I strolled into a coffee shop, I was chancing a meeting with a producer or a writer. Kids I went to school with had parents in the industry, and going over to their houses meant potentially being discovered. Opportunity was everywhere, and I held onto that belief for a little too long. Maybe that's the reason I'm in this position—I got cocky and lazy and left my entire life up to chance. I expected New York to do its thing *for* me."

"Still better than doing nothing at all," she said. Her skin had returned to its normal color, imbued with an angelic glow. "I hate to be a typical small-town girl, but the rumors are true: It's scary to leave. Not only that, it's hard. I make good money for my area, but I don't make good money anywhere else in the country. Not in the places that matter, anyway. Like you, I don't have much in the way of education or experience. I pigeonholed myself as a waitress." She gave a small laugh. "And I'm angry at my dad for refusing to keep living that way. To be quiet, to not take up any space in the world, to lead his minuscule existence. I don't know. I guess I just thought maybe he'd wanna take his daughter along for that. Why leave me behind to be nothing nowhere?"

As she spoke, I watched the way lines formed on her complexion. I saw the little divots in her cheeks, almost dimples, but not quite. I watched the stray hairs flutter across her forehead, glinting in the dim overhead lighting. I saw her eyelashes caress the tops of her brows and the way her lips moved as she formed letters. Words.

"I like you a lot better this way," I said, regretting it as it came out of my mouth. I thought it was rude.

"Really?" she replied, but there wasn't a hint of annoyance in her voice or upset. Only intrigue.

"Yeah. Open. I like... I like hearing about your life."

"The only person who would say that is a man on a date desperately trying to get into a girl's pants," she rebuffed.

"I wouldn't have to try that hard," I snickered, "the bathroom's right there. We can do it right now."

"Really?" she asked again, her expression like a dare.

I was about to get up from my seat, seizing the opportunity, when—

"I don't sleep with people on the first date."

"It's not our first," I replied quickly, now fearing that she hadn't been as serious as I was. Something about her was enticing, intoxicating... I wanted to whisk her away right then and there.

"You're right," she said, genuinely contemplating the logic. "Alright. I'll meet you there."

"What?" I was a bit bewildered.

"First stall." And she sauntered away from the table, her hips swaying with a momentum that couldn't have been anything other than intentional.

I followed after her like a puppy, my heart racing with anticipation. If only I could have started to strip on my way over, lapping up the opportunity with an overt enthusiasm that surely would have put her off. Right. I had to stay cool and be suave. She was expecting a devilish tryst, something to break the monotony of her previously unremarkable life. Was she choosing me out of convenience? To wear me like a badge when she returned to Virginia? I wanted to be more than just a brief story in her life. But those worries were for another day.

Johnny had disappeared into the kitchen, and none of the other staff were due to arrive for a while. When I pushed into the bathroom, Abigail was waiting for me in the open stall, just as she had promised. She'd taken off her sweater and hung it over the door, revealing a black, ill-fitting bra that did more for me and my desires than her own comfort. I lingered a bit too long, the sight of her delicate collarbones and her shapely waist stopping me in my tracks.

"Is something wrong?" she asked, her voice on the border of embarrassment.

"Of course not." I licked my lips. "I just don't know where to start."

"So kiss me."

And I did. I tackled her with my mouth, pressing her soft skin into my face, my hands, my thighs. I pinned her against the wall, allowing my fingers to run the length of her torso, snapping the button of her jeans out of place in the process. I felt ravenous, inhaling the scent of her freshly washed hair and her natural musk. It drove me wild, compelling me to speed up a process I wanted to savor.

"What are you doing to me?" I breathlessly asked as I unlooped my belt.

She took me in her hands, and I gasped, my skin growing hotter still. "Fucking you," she replied with a sensuous giggle.

Then I was inside of her, and I swore I was about to die.

***

Abigail was throwing her sweater over her back the moment it was over. She clumsily ran her fingers through her hair, attempting to smooth what had gotten rumpled. I was still in a daze, sitting on the toilet without a care as I watched her get ready to leave.

"I have your number," she said. I thought the announcement was curt. But she kissed me before she fled, her lips still perfumed with the scent of me. Of us.

Once I could steadily stand on my two feet, I sauntered out to the stage, picked up my guitar, and sang in earnest. I fashioned the words as soon as they came to me, and I amplified them to the still-empty room. It was a song for Abigail, no doubt. What a peculiar, beautiful woman.

Chapter 7:

Abigail

I lay on the bed, my belly to the mattress, as I dialled the only person in the world who could entertain what I was about to say. I typed in her number by heart, making a mental note to add her as a contact when I hung up and waited impatiently as the line rang.

What are you doing to me? Paolo's words echoed in my ears. I didn't know. I felt like I had done something wrong like I had rushed something on a whim, and now I'd never be able to show my face around Belmont's again. In an effort to be spontaneous, I acted on a feeling I wanted to be buried deep within my chest, not wrapped around my body. It was good, though. So good. I felt myself blushing, my legs squirming, as the other line finally clicked.

"Stacey!" I shouted into the receiver, relieved to be talking to my best friend.

"Abby?" she asked tenderly.

"Yes! Ugh, sorry, you were probably worried sick about me," I started, not giving her the space to get in a word. "I lost my phone! Well, it was stolen really, and then this guy—I have to tell you about him—gave me money to buy a new one. So, save this number. I think I'll be stuck with it for a while."

"Oh, Abby," she sobbed.

I was tempted to laugh it off, to believe that she had been so worried about my absence that she had worked herself up. Maybe she'd even filed a report with the police, and they chuckled as she announced I was in a whole other state. One where people went missing all the time. Or ran away to. They told her I had up and left her without saying goodbye. No wonder she was in tears. But I couldn't help but think that something else was wrong, too. It was unlike Stacey to even get so riled up in the first place, to make herself sick over my fate. She cared about me, that was certain, but to have a meltdown? Odd.

"I have some bad news," she said, and my heart dropped.

"Are you... are you okay?"

"Yeah. I mean..." Her voice broke. "She's sick, Abigail."

"Who? Momma?"

"Yeah."

"Well, I know that," I replied, attempting to pad the truth. The eventual reveal. Of course, she wasn't as sick as I'd left her. Stacey wasn't calling me just to make me feel guilty about my trip.

"She's dying, Abby."

***

Paolo pulled up to the hotel in a Subaru—the seats had been covered in plush faux fur, and the dashboard speckled with coffee stains and stickers. Clearly, this was not his vehicle. But he hopped out of the driver's side as soon as he approached, snapping up my bags and gently placing them in the trunk. Then he opened my door for me and ensured that I was buckled before he plunged into the Manhattan traffic.

"Are you sure we'll make it to the airport on time?" I asked in a hoarse voice. As soon as Stacey and I got off the phone, the waterworks came. The sobbing, the labored breathing, the wailing into my pillow. I cranked the air conditioner and the volume on the TV just to drown out the noise. I didn't want any visits to my room or calls from the front desk. I wanted to be left alone.

"Of course," Paolo replied, the usual arrogance in his cadence dissipated. "I'll move heaven and earth to make that happen."

"Even if I catch the plane," I sighed, "I might be late, anyway."

"It's that bad, huh?" he asked quietly, his eyes squarely on the road. We jerked as he took his foot on and off the brakes, inching his way through the crowded lanes and attempting to bully others into giving him space.

"If I had just sold the bar..." I began, but I knew it was a farce. There was no saving my Momma from her untimely demise. I could have sold 15 bars and still wouldn't have been able to keep her afloat for much longer. This was beyond medicine and doctors. "She's in the hospital," I continued, "she hasn't been this bad in a while, and I guess the nurses are saying to, you know, make sure everything's prepared. That we have all the arrangements."

"I'm sorry."

"And Stacey tried to tell me about it, too, but I didn't have my fucking phone. I was... hours away from losing her. If I hadn't reached out, I wouldn't be rushing to her bedside, and I'd be kicking myself at her funeral."

"I'm sure she would have understood."

For some reason, the casual insistence was grating to me. He didn't know my mother. Hell, he hardly knew me. He probably thought this was a favor he could cash in on, and his kindness was merely a means to an end. Who did this guy think he was, and why did I keep falling for his bullshit?

"No, she wouldn't," I protested. "I allowed her to die alone so I could have sex with strangers in New York City."

"You didn't come here for me," he shot back, his defenses creeping up.

"Exactly, and yet here I am, wasting her final moments with you. Leading you into bathrooms while she's dying. If you had just let me stay on task, this wouldn't have been an issue."

"It sounds like you're blaming me—"

"Maybe I am. So what?"

"So I don't want to be a part of this."

"And I wanted to be involved in your little scheme? You fucked with my life, Paolo, for a silly bar and your pathetic music."

"Oh, I'm pathetic now."

"You always have been."

I sank further into the seat, not wanting to look at him or be in his vicinity. Open my body up to him. The stench of the perfumed car was making me nauseous. I just wanted to be home already, to see my mother for the last time and get it over with. Though I knew I had to relish every remaining second we had together, I also didn't want to draw out the suffering any longer. Make it quick. Make it count. Paolo didn't understand value if it didn't revolve around his selfish performance. At least, that's what I assumed, anyway.

"You know, I'm trying to help you," he snapped.

"Yeah, look at all the good you've done me."

The rest of our trip was silent, and as soon as his tires squealed into the airport drop-off, I stormed out of the car. This time, he didn't try to help me with my bags. He sat in the driver's seat, his knuckles white on the steering wheel, and tore out of the airport the second I was through the sliding glass doors. *Good,* I thought. *It was better this way.*

✳✳✳

The orchestra of machines reverberated throughout the sterile room. Momma was alone when I arrived, not a single gift or card, save for the offerings brought by Stacey, decorated her hospital bed. This would be where she died, and it didn't even look comforting. There was no love or hope, only the morose atmosphere that reeked of isolation and disease.

She tried to turn her head to look at me, but Momma was practically in a coffin, the confines of which were invisible to me but felt by her ailing body. I sat by her side, stroking her soft, wrinkled hands as I reminded her that I was there. Always there. Just like she had been for me.

"My beautiful girl," she crooned, one pupil landing on my stricken face.

"It's been a while, Momma," I replied, using my free hand to wipe her forehead with a damp towel. She wasn't sweating or shaking, but I imagined it was nice to be taken care of, no matter how vain it all was.

"Back from the big city," she said with a smile.

"Yeah. Yeah, I am."

"Isn't it just wonderful?"

"Not as good as home."

"Pfft," she huffed and mustered the strength to crane her neck fully. "Don't you lie to me now, Abigail."

"I'm not lying," I insisted. I was a little shocked by the revelation—had my mother wanted to follow Dad to New York? Was that why she was never angry? Had she encouraged his flight, jealous only that she didn't have it in her to make such a drastic lifestyle change? "I miss the peace of the countryside. I miss the way it smells... all that clean air."

"You don't need to pretend we're in some sorta paradise over here, my sweets. We got just as much pollution, crud, and nastiness as they do. Maybe even worse, 'cause everyone's faking like it's not true."

"I—"

But she cut me off. "Just tell me about your adventures, Abigail. Tell me something good."

"Nothing happened to me, Momma."

"I want my daughter to have an interesting life."

I sighed. "I mean, I did... I did meet this guy."

"Oh, wow," she gasped. Always a romantic, I knew my mother would appreciate a love story.

"He's handsome. Like, really handsome. And very generous. He sings at Daddy's bar most evenings. He does so good at it that it's his full-time job." I looked at her for her input, but her eyes were closed. She was drifting off listening to my voice, so I continued. "He's also a gentleman—he wants to help me either sell or fix up Belmont's. He knows how much it means to people and how much it could mean to me. I guess I never forgave Daddy for leaving, but I think I'm the only one still holding onto that. He left me something I can actually, you know, build a life on. I can either move to New York and run a business or cash in and make a home elsewhere with the profits. And Pa—this guy, well, he wants to help me do that, and I don't know why. That must be his nature.

"I thought, at first, he saw me as nothing more than a stray puppy. I lost my phone. I didn't have anywhere to sleep, and I was all frazzled. Just a huge mess. But he got me a hotel room, ensured I had the money to get a new phone, and should all that have failed he was ready to put me up in his own house. Nothing to gain from it. Pure kindness... Anyway, I don't know if I'll see him again or ever go back there. It was intense. I didn't feel good, you know? I missed home. I missed you."

"Of course you missed me, Abigail," she said as she patted my hand with hers. "And I missed you, too. Terribly. I'll always miss you. I'm your mother. That doesn't mean you should hold yourself back."

"But look at what happens when I leave." I was crying now, and so was she. We both knew that what was trickling through her system was taking her life before my very eyes. Her voice had grown coarser in the brief moments I had been by her side. She was fading fast.

"That's not a good enough reason to stay, my girl. You need to be bigger and better than me. You need to follow your heart."

"What if I don't know how to do that?"

"Trust yourself," she said, her grip loosening on my clasped hand.

The machines were winding down, the endless whirring and noise dissipating as her chest heaved one final time. As she slipped into the abyss, the flatline of her heart emanated throughout the room like a death knell. Nurses rushed in to revive her, but it was a fruitless attempt and one I didn't appreciate. I just wanted to be alone with her while her skin was still warm and the remnants of life were still in her cheeks. As Momma had said, the worst thing a person could do was pretend. Everyone knew there was no coming back, so why did they bother?

Just leave us alone, I silently pleaded. *Leave us alone.*

Chapter 8:

Paolo

The energy in the building was hostile as I wrapped up my set, the audience before me crossing their arms and pouting at my continued playing. I perspired as I watched their faces drop and their conversations continue, their voices happily drowning out my words as I faded into the background of their lives. I wondered if there was signage outside that denoted another musician was meant to perform, and that's why they were so aggravated by my presence. I had never received such a vile reaction, not even when I was fresh-faced and still learning how to construct a song.

My material was new, yes, and untested by an audience, but there was no way it was so terrible that I wasn't deserving of these people's attention. If anything, my style had matured—my writing was more careful and considerate in its poetic scheme, my chord progressions were complex, and my voice had been trained to land every note with reliable accuracy. I was better, no doubt, than when I was at my label, and yet their attitudes did not reflect this abject reality.

After a brisk bout of forced applause, I strutted off the stage, trying not to look as scorned as I felt. My phone was ringing incessantly in my pocket, the vibrations adding to my irritation as it lit up my leg. Gritting my teeth, I finally answered, only to be met with sobs on the other end. It was Abigail, and though she had returned to New York, she didn't seem to be in high spirits about it.

"Can you pick me up?" she asked as soon as she heard my breathing on the other end of the line.

I wasn't in the mood to be used by this woman. "Why on earth would I do that?"

"What?" she sounded genuinely confused.

"Do you want to berate me again? Are there some insults you still haven't gotten off your chest?"

"Paolo, I didn't mean to."

"Didn't mean to what? Ask me for help over and over again just to spit in my face?"

"Please, Paolo." I felt myself weakening. "Let me make it up to you."

"How?" My shoulders had grown slack, the tension I was holding melting as her effortless cadence drifted into my ears. I knew she was lying or trying to manipulate me into cooperating. She didn't like me as much as I didn't like her, and yet we were engaged in some masochistic tug-of-war.

"I'll apologize."

"Big deal," I scoffed, trying to hide the intrigue in my tone.

"And more."

***

And there I was, parked at the airport, craning my neck to look for Abigail amidst the swathes of people. I was an adult. I should have known better than to put myself in this position. Perhaps I wanted to be chastised, to feel the full weight of my failure from tonight's performance. I wanted to hear how terrible and awful I was, to confirm the insecurities that had been roving through my mind as of late. I had to make my self-doubt real by forcing it to drip off the lips of the most beautiful woman I had ever seen.

When her moon-like features finally appeared, I unlocked the car and opened the passenger door, hopelessly unable to conceal my grin as her cheeks took on a rosy hue at the sight of me. Even with her puffy eyes, messy hair, and wrinkled clothing, she was a vision. She had less luggage with her this time and threw a military duffle bag into the backseat without asking permission, which I struggled not to comment on. I knew a fight was on the horizon; we couldn't help but bicker, but

I didn't want to start the rounds just yet. We needed a few minutes to settle in, at least.

"Thank you, Paolo," she cooed as she placed a hand on my thigh. I thought I read seduction on her features, but I tried to push the thought aside. She was vulnerable and confused, not looking for another escapade. "I'm really sorry," she continued, using her other hand to brush strands of my hair behind my ear.

But then she was leaning forward, the scent of her homely soap infiltrating my senses as she drew near. Her lips parted, and suddenly, they were on mine, gently prodding me until I opened up. Until I accepted her. Then I was feeling ravenous, that same lustful, consuming frenzy taking over as we fell deeper into the kiss. I heard the zipper of her jeans unlatch, and then she grabbed my hand, groping her breast to the space between her thighs.

"I want you so bad, Paolo," she crooned, guiding me to the places she wanted to be touched.

"Not here," I replied, "I'm taking you home."

***

The drive back to my apartment was brutal. Abigail had started shedding layers, exposing her pale, delicate shoulders, her luscious cleavage, and her convulsing midriff. Luckily, there was hardly any traffic—I knew the city well enough to enter through Brooklyn and take the less traveled, inner-city highways. Abigail thrashed in the front seat, pleasuring herself with her eyes focused on me. It pained me to break her gaze, to occasionally watch the road for the sake of getting to my bedroom in one piece.

Sometimes, she would reach over and pet me, her grasp teasing as her fingers drifted to my crotch and lingered but never alleviated my throbbing member. I felt like I was bursting at the seams, my excitement becoming violent as I desperately wanted to be satisfied. I almost wanted to beg her to put her hands on it, her mouth, her tongue, but I also didn't want to spoil the evening ahead of us.

When I finally managed to find a place to park outside my building, I rushed out of the car, barely putting it in park as I raced to open her door. We left her luggage on the backseat, and she followed me inside the foyer, her hands tugging at my shirt, at my belt, at my arms, as I fumbled with the keys. I dragged her to the elevator, and that's when she undid my pants, slipping her slender fingers under my clothes and stroking my pulsating cock. I moaned, and her lips matched my gape, her tongue flicking the inside of my mouth as I struggled to stay afloat, to stay lucid. I was in heaven. I led her to my bedroom out of habit rather than sight, my vision thick with the haze of lust. She barely let me come up for air, her mouth moving over mine with sensual desperation. I was lost in her gravitational pull, our lips syncing in torrid unison.

Luckily, none of the lights were on in the apartment, and my parents weren't awake. We could make as much noise as we wanted. I playfully nudged Abigail onto the bed, ripping off her jeans as she slid back on the mattress, her legs splaying out to expose herself to me. She was dripping, her heavenly liquid pooling on the blanket beneath her. I dove right in, my tongue finding her hottest points and lapping them up, and my hands reaching across her torso until they found her full breasts. She was soft and warm, the groans emanating from her throat primal yet feminine. I knew she finished when her legs ceased to quake, and her spine fell flat against the bed, so I climbed on top of her, kissing her so she could taste herself.

I tore off my shirt and let her ogle me, her lips drawn back in a smirk as she traced the outline of my abs. My engorged penis had burst from my jeans, and I rubbed it while she watched, while she joined me by putting her mouth on it between strokes. I wanted to keep going, to keep the memory of Abigail praising my loins alive for as long as possible, but neither of us could take it anymore.

I was inside of her again, pumping slowly and sensually, elongating the activity with my careful passion. I felt the cum rush to the tip of my sensitive member, threatening to unleash too soon, but the sight of Abigail's suddenly disgruntled expression shot me off my high horse.

"What's wrong?" I asked, embarrassment creeping in.

"Harder," she begged, grabbing my backside and trying to command my penis.

I thrust faster, but my tempo didn't seem to match her desires. She struggled to position me to feel me against her walls the way she wanted. The more we failed to fall into step, the less I wanted to finish and the more flustered she became. Until she was crying. Awkwardly, I slid off her, unsure whether it was my performance that was upsetting her or something else. I was hoping for the latter, and as she turned away from me but didn't leave the bed, I felt my suspicions had been confirmed.

"I'm sorry," she sobbed, the peak of her flush cheek poking at me in the darkness. I knew she had lifted her head up enough to steal a glance at my broken countenance. "It's not you..."

"Okay. I mean, are you sure? I don't want you to think... or for this to be..." I couldn't find my bearings, as I was guilty and uncomfortable all at once.

"My mom died," she admitted, her tears flowing faster now.

Shit, I thought to myself. I had jumped at the opportunity to sleep with the girl who had lost both her parents in a matter of weeks and was clearly attempting to work through her grief in a strange, disembodied way. Was I a terrible person? Had I taken advantage of her?

"I'm sorry," I offered.

"For what?" she whimpered in reply.

"For your loss. Your losses. For having sex with you."

"Don't apologize for that." She whirled around and met me once again. "I wanted it."

"Did you?"

"Of course. This wasn't some, like, fucked up act of mourning. It's not like I have a dead husband you remind me of."

"I don't know..." I trailed off, once again humiliated by my actions, no matter how innocent or desired they were.

"Very Freudian of you to think I'm horny over the loss of my parents," she added with a laugh. I joined her, craving the levity I had been riding only a few short minutes ago. "I'm sorry," she repeated.

"Don't be."

"I made it weird."

"You didn't."

"I should probably go."

"Don't." And I meant it. I didn't want her to leave. I liked the warmth of her body and the sound of her sniffles. I liked the way she evened out my lumpy mattress and the smell of her sweat in my hair and on my pillows. Despite our less-than-ideal encounter, I didn't want her to be alone.

"I just—I know I'm old, but like, doesn't this make me an orphan? And I know I wasn't close with my dad—toward the end, I didn't even know him—but that doesn't mean I don't miss him. You go through life thinking your parents are invincible like it's impossible to exist without them being around in some capacity. As long as they're on earth, so are you, but... they're gone. I have nobody. I feel like this means I'm not a real person anymore."

"That's not true," I murmured, stroking her forehead as she spoke. "You have me."

"Really?"

"Of course."

She rolled over again, this time bringing her body close to mine and allowing me to throw an arm across her chest. I pulled her tight to me, pressing her skin into mine until our bodies had fully melted together. I was her, and she was me. I waited for her to doze off, recognizing the heaviness of her breath as she blew air onto my arm, and once I was certain she was okay, I closed my eyes, too.

Chapter 9:

Abigail

My eyes fluttered open as the morning sun infiltrated our private space. Paolo's chin was nuzzled into the crook of my neck, and my hand was gently pressed into the base of his skull. We breathed in harmony, our lungs expanding and contracting at the same time, and I felt safe. I wanted to be embarrassed about my behavior last night—not only had I burst into tears at the worst possible moment, but I inadvertently hurt Paolo by making him believe that he had done something terrible to me. I had taken vulnerability to a new extreme, and I wasn't sure how I felt about it, but he had shown me so much compassion. I wasn't confident that my take on the events was exactly accurate. I obviously hadn't pushed him away, right? If he was grossed out by my sensitivity and lack of decorum, he would have taken me up on my offer to leave. I didn't want to be the girl who didn't know how to take a hint, but I also didn't want to spoil this moment by getting inside my head and convincing myself that this good thing was actually a disaster in waiting. Right?

Enjoy it while it lasts, I tried to tell myself. But my ability to let go, to immerse myself in the moment, was quickly disrupted. Paolo's door burst open, and across the threshold stepped a middle-aged woman holding a wicker basket full of laundry. She didn't immediately clock my presence, giving me time to assess her features, which looked strikingly like Paolo's. She rifled through his dresser beside the door for a moment, throwing clothes into their respective places as she had so evidently done a million times before.

"Mom?" Paolo's tired voice rasped from beside me.

Now we were making eye contact, her eyes bulging out of her skull as she took me in. I pulled the covers over my exposed breasts, suddenly aware of the state I was in. I wanted to hide. I wanted to run away.

"Sorry, Son," she whispered hastily and skirted out of the room, leaving a trail of laundry in her wake.

"You live with your parents?" I asked Paolo once the coast was clear. He sighed, and that was all the confirmation I needed.

Flinging off the covers, I dressed as quickly as I could, making peace with the fact that I couldn't find my bra or my left sock. They weren't important anymore. I just needed to get the hell out of there.

"Where are you going?" he asked, still sitting on the bed. His inaction infuriated me for some reason.

"To my hotel," I huffed, making sure no part of my body was visible through my clothing. "I need my stuff out of your car."

"Are you mad at me?" The question seemed so childish, given our circumstances.

"I don't know." *Should I be?*

"I can explain."

"Explain what? You're—" I didn't want to say it. I didn't want to be mean. I was tired of fighting with him. He showed me grace last night, so why couldn't I do the same? What compelled me to keep stoking a fire that had long burnt out? I was playing in the ashes of our fury, hoping the embers would come back to life. "You're a grown man mooching off his parents." I said it. I completed the sentence. Another strike in our already imperfect track record.

So he let me go. I heard him mutter something about triggering the locking mechanism on the car from his window. When I got to the Subaru, the doors conceded to my grasp without any trouble. I grabbed my stuff and hurried off in a random direction. I just wanted to be anywhere else.

***

The buyer was stalking around the bar again, her expression just as dark as the first time. Perpetually unimpressed, I began to question why she was here in the first place. Surely, the trouble she would have to go through in order to renovate the building wasn't worth the end result. How could she anticipate making much money off a project that was inevitably going to take years to complete? And the payment she was offering me... It was an obscene sum to give to a girl who didn't know any better, who would have accepted less and thought she had struck gold. Perhaps Belmont's was worth more than I realized, and my efforts to rid myself of it was the foolish act, not whatever the buyer was doing.

I wished I had someone to consult. The lawyer was the one pulling the strings, and clearly, he felt this was the best move; otherwise, he wouldn't have put me in this position. He wasn't some fatherly figure who had operated in the background of my life, watching me grow and blossom and hoping this final test would push me in the right direction. He was a faceless figure who crunched numbers and mulled over the objectives. He was focused on pragmatic, unemotional work.

Paolo, on the other hand, operated solely on passion. His desire for Belmont's to remain a fixture in the neighborhood was not because he had some altruistic vision or a keen sense for business but because he had a connection with the place. It was his haven, a space where he could perform, let loose, and forget his particular circumstances. He wasn't the guy who still lived with his parents when he was on stage— he was the brooding musician who appeared only to sing his melodies and then vanish into the crowd, where his anonymity enabled him to gather more material for his work. Belmont's provided him the cover by which to subsume an alternate personality, a different life, a sense of purpose that left him as soon as he crossed the threshold into his childhood bedroom.

I feared that I had been too harsh on him. Clearly, he was down on his luck, and rubbing that fact into his face wasn't going to help him and his predicament very much. If anything, he'd probably fall deeper into his despair, rebuilding his misery on the pillars of my disdain and wearing his living situation as a badge of honor. If a woman truly loved him, truly cared about him, she would look the other way. He wouldn't be emboldened to move out on his own, to finally test his limits. No, he'd stubbornly root himself in place, insisting that it was everyone else who was the problem and not him. That's always how men operated, anyway. Selfish, moronic, and hostile to their own growth. Paolo was no different.

Then again, I didn't like how bitter I became when I thought of him. I didn't like how I behaved when I was around him. Something about his presence opened me up like a zipper, exposing my innards and my depths, making public my feelings and wants. The vulnerability was discomforting, and instead of embracing it, I turned it into something sinister. Something to be angry about. I couldn't see the beauty in the person he'd been making me, for I didn't understand what made him deserving of it. Why him? The man-child who manipulated me for his own gain. The crazed lover who didn't live up to expectations.

That was another thing: The sex had been disappointing. I did my best to turn myself on, to get the both of us riled up, but when it came time for him to perform, he just couldn't sync our bodies. Spiritually, we seemed to agree, but physically, we were out of touch. Why couldn't he hate me the way I wanted him to? Why couldn't he take that rage out on my body, pounding me into the headboard until I saw visions of angels and Gods? Another reason why his ability to unravel and expose me bothered me so much—ultimately, he didn't know what to do with me. He didn't understand what he saw, what he prodded at, what he coaxed out of me. I was still a mystery to be solved, but I was tired of having to explain myself. A real man would have taken charge, would have innately understood what needed to be done. I didn't want to be the one to encourage Paolo to mature. I wanted to be the one to receive the fruits of someone else's labor. I wanted to be with Paolo the man, not the budding flower.

"I'll take it," the buyer announced, her voice cutting through my thoughts.

"Oh," was all I could manufacture for a reply.

"Is that alright?"

"I—"

"My offer still stands. Twenty percent over asking."

"I just... I have to run the numbers by my people," I lied. I needed to buy more time. "I think they're great, but I'm not the only one invested in Belmont's. We'll be in touch."

***

Paolo was onstage. He serenaded the microphone, but it wasn't coming out right. I wasn't the only one who felt that way—the crowd around me was unimpressed. Arms were across chests, and scowls were worn on faces. With drinks on hand, they should have at least been pleasantly subdued, but the aggressively off-kilter music was distracting. Disrupting.

He hadn't noticed me when he walked in. Or maybe he did and simply chose to ignore me. Either way, I had been sitting in the darkness for hours, nursing beer after beer as Johnny, who was finally warming up to me, plied me with alcohol. He kept my glass full and my table clean, and I thanked him with the knowledge of my delayed transaction. Perhaps he was also operating on his own agenda, hoping to force my hand with cold beers into letting him keep his job. I wasn't trying to hurt these people, though. I was just trying to move on with my life. What was wrong with that?

Paolo's present failure was weighing on me, though. I couldn't continue to wallow in my corner, watching as he struggled through song after song. Didn't he see the looks on their worn faces? Didn't he want to impress them? To garner fans? He was wasting his life on his ambition, only to refuse to adapt to his audience; to actually make them like him.

Then, I was on my feet, strolling over to the stage with the confidence of someone who was meant to be there. As if I knew what I was doing. Like it was planned, there was a break in the set, and I joined him on stage, grabbing the extra microphone that sat on a stand beside him. He shot daggers into me, but to kick me off the stage would have been a bigger embarrassment than simply letting me sing. Because I *was* singing. I knew all the words. Having listened to Paolo play, I had ingested his lyrics without even realizing it, and now I was regurgitating them to a crowd, effortlessly spinning them until I saw hands move to chins and smiles creep along faces. He joined me occasionally, our harmony natural as we finally fell into the rhythm. To suggest it wasn't magical would be a disservice to our duet.

A love like ours,

Don't come around too often.

A love like ours,

Is off the tracks before you can stop it.

I know you now, but I knew you then,

A million lifetimes behind us,

And still, you're my only friend.

A love like ours,

Burns bright, but it always dies.

A love like ours,

Is breaking my heart,

All the time.

As we uttered the words, I felt them in my bones. They were true. Honest. Paolo opened me up because this wasn't the first time he had known me, and it wouldn't be the last. We were drawn to each other like heroes in a novel, and perhaps this would be the end for our current bodies—I could see the unrelenting frustration on his face; the reality of my inevitable sale was looming over us, but we'd find each other again. Spiritually, we were intertwined.

Chapter 10:

Paolo

The applause was unmistakable, even as I tried to ignore it while storming off the stage. It had become a habit of mine to exit in a fury, but this time, I had Abigail by the hand, and I was dragging her into my storm. People stood up from their seats as we walked by, and Abigail waved as though she were a princess receiving her flowers. My head grew hot the more the praise continued, my ire with Abigail increasing as she flattered what should have been my adoring fans. I was a solo act with a vision and sound of my own, and I wasn't about to share it with someone else. I didn't want a partnership. I wanted to be recognized on my own terms, for my own merits.

She followed me without question, even as I exited the bar and hurled her into the alleyway. We were surrounded by overflowing garbage bins and the distant conversations of people walking by. In the darkness, though, we could be alone. Hidden by the shadows of the buildings that surrounded us, melded together into a formless, indiscernible mass.

I kissed her. For all my anger and all my feelings of betrayal, I still wanted her. Maybe this was how I would show her what I was made of. She brought me into her warmth, returning my kiss with the same level of enthusiasm. She pulled the hairs at the nape of my neck, taking charge of our mouths as I worked on my boner. It wasn't long before I was hard and ready to go. Luckily, Abigail was wearing a skirt—pulling her panties down to her knees, I pushed myself inside of her, moaning in the process. She always felt so good. Her legs were wrapped around my waist as I thrust into her, enjoying the way her walls seemed to suction onto cock like they didn't want me to leave.

"Oh, Paolo," she whispered in my ear. Her tongue flicked my lobes, her teeth lightly gnawing on the skin. The sensation sent shivers down my spine, and I couldn't hold it any longer. I burst inside of her.

✳✳✳

We sat at a secluded booth, our mugs filled with only water as we gazed at each other, unsure of what to say first. Did I want to be the one to admit that our sex was only good when we knew we shouldn't be doing it? There had to be a layer of transgression in order for our desires to align. I felt sick yet satisfied, plotting our next romp as I struggled to maintain my composure. I wondered what it would be like to make love in Central Park late at night or under the table at a restaurant. I wondered how she'd clench with more eyes on us, how that friction would feel against my swollen member.

"That was nice," she said finally.

"The sex?" I replied with a grin.

"No." My smile dropped. "The song."

"Oh... right." My bubble had burst. "I, uh, I disagree."

"What? Why?" Her voice had a slight giggle to it, as though she assumed my repulsion was purely in jest. She prepped herself for another bout of foul-mouthed foreplay, but I wasn't trying to arouse her. I was just being honest.

"I don't do duets," I said sternly.

"Come on," she retorted, but the light had drained from her countenance.

"I don't. I think I'm allowed to dictate my own music."

"I'm not trying to be added to your roster."

"And I'm not looking for notes on my songs."

"I think you should reconsider that."

"Why?"

She shrugged, the sourness on her tongue rearing its ugly head with a *cluck*. "They hate you."

"The audience? Or you?"

"Don't turn this around on me. You know as well as I do they weren't feeling your music."

"No, they weren't interested in my sound. It's not for everyone, and I'm okay with that. I don't need broad appeal or whatever it was you were trying to do."

"I was helping you."

"You don't know shit about music, you don't know shit about singing. Maybe the nerves, the adrenaline; it saved your ass up there tonight. But I have an ear for this kind of thing—"

"I don't need to be berated. I'm not some bright-eyed girl standing in your office begging for a chance, okay? I'm no star, I get it, and I don't want to be. But you're clearly directionless and need some kind of breath of fresh air. Doesn't need to be me, but on your own, you're just not cutting it."

"Wow, sage advice from the bereaved."

"What does that have to do with anything?"

"You're obviously, you know—" I spun my fingers around my head, a juvenile attempt to insult her. It was a move I knew I'd regret later.

"Crazy! You think I'm crazy! All because I sang a couple lyrics."

"They weren't yours to sing! What kind of person does that?"

"Ever heard of karaoke?"

"So, that's all this is to you? A cute little show, a silly performance. Something to brag about for a few weeks. But it's my career you're fucking with."

She pushed her hair back with her palms, resting her elbows on the table and staring at the pools of water that had collected around our glasses. She shook her head. "I don't know why we're fighting about this."

"Sorry, you don't have anything in your life worth fighting for, Abigail."

"Stop," she said. Her voice was a whisper now, the strength depleted from her register. "Paolo, please..."

"You can't just cry to get out of everything."

"That's not what I'm doing."

"Oh really? What about last night?"

"Stop!" Her eyes were wild, her emotions a wreck underneath the pristine surface of a complexion. She was engaged in a losing battle, with an inability to communicate with me and yet an insatiable desire to try. I was tired of this, too. What were we doing? "You're trying to push me away, and it's not going to work, alright? For better or for worse, I think we like each other, and I think that—"

"I don't like you." I don't know why I said it. It rolled off my tongue so easily, without caution or contemplation. If I slipped into the phrase so effortlessly, I must have meant it.

"Well," she replied flatly. Her entire body stiffened. "Okay, then. That settles it." She paused, but I refused to fill the silence. "I'm selling the bar."

My blood boiled once again. "Real nice threat, Abigail. You don't get what you want, so you take it out on everyone else."

"This isn't a threat. I got an offer. It's way beyond reasonable, so I'm taking it."

"You can't do that."

"Oh, fuck *off*, Paolo. I don't know you. I don't owe you my life. I want out of here, I want away from this bar, and so that's what I'm doing.

I'm helping myself. Isn't that what you're doing with your music? Fuck everybody else. Just do what you want, how you want. So I don't need a lecture, or another bargaining chip, or a slew of insults coming out of your dirty mouth. The world doesn't revolve around you."

She got up to leave, and I felt the urge to stop her, to apologize, but I couldn't give in to my weakness. We were bad for each other; it was obvious. Why continue to chase a woman who had no problem sinking me? She'd overhaul my music, rip up my stage, and usurp my fanbase, only to deny it later. She'd claim that I was delusional and self-centered, and then we'd bicker until we devolved into tears. It was a pathetic merry-go-round.

"Are you happy that you've crushed me, Abigail?" I asked, unable to fully prevent my speech from forming.

"All I've tried to do is make it work with you."

"Really? 'Cause this doesn't feel like work to me."

She rolled her eyes, and with her purse over her shoulder, she marched out of the bar. I wondered if that would be the last time I saw her, and the idea of leaving it on a bad note made my stomach curdle. I was annoyed by my own inability to parse through my emotions, struggling to decide whether I hated this woman or not. Would it have made a difference if I was sure, though?

***

Back at home, my parents had been quietly tiptoeing around me, nervous to send another guest packing. My mother had been apologetic, but my father insisted this was a sign from the Lord that I needed to grow up. They remarked how beautiful she was, which I found to be a disturbing comment considering how they found her, but they lamented our *perfect appearance* as a couple anyway. Their enthusiasm for Abigail only depressed me more. Was I wrong for letting her go? Maybe my parents saw something in her that I couldn't—I was so immersed in my own woes that I failed to see what else she offered. She was either a woman to bed or an enemy to accost.

But, despite our disagreements, she had been a fascinating woman. I had known from the moment I laid eyes on her that she was special in some kind of ethereal, intangible way. I secretly wanted to uncover more of her history, and I pondered searching her name on Google to yield that result. What I had imploded, I could steal back in some small, insignificant way. A victory that would be all mine. It wasn't the same, though. I wanted to hear the words on her tongue, not watch them pixelate on a computer screen.

And then my hand was grasped around a pen, and my thoughts were floating over a page in my notebook. I was putting my insecurities in writing, my queries in prose, and I released myself of those nagging ramblings. I recounted our passion, our undeniable chemistry. Our fallout, our detestation. I lashed out at her because she scared me—she reminded me that I was fallible, that my career could be taken away from me for banal and impersonal reasons. She instilled me with rage because I felt weak in her presence—I was a man living with his parents, ignorantly clinging to a dream that should have long been dead and blaming her when she somehow posed a threat to it. But I was erroneously pointing a finger, trying to make her the enemy because it was easier to hate an outside force rather than contend with my own shortcomings. Somebody did this to me. I didn't do it to myself.

That had gotten me nowhere, though. I was still without a respectable job, without an apartment to call my own, and a girlfriend to cheer me on. I had terrorized the only woman I had ever loved, and yes, I had loved her because I was too childish to do anything else. Perhaps admitting now that I didn't have my own best interests at heart would be the start of my metamorphosis. As I fixed my attitude and adjusted my behavior, I'd think back to Abigail and everything I could've had if I had just been a better person. I think I'd heard my whole life that it was better to love and lose, and maybe that's what had gone on here. She was a lesson I'd be learning over and over again until I finally struck out on my own, called a woman my wife, and grew the fuck up. Then again, there was beauty in exaggeration—maybe she was only meant to inspire a few more songs.

Chapter 11:

Abigail

I wandered through the winding cement pathways of Central Park, hoping to finally lose myself in the natural world and always coming up short. The tires whirring along the pavement infiltrated every tree branch, and my thoughts continued to be punctuated by the voices of passersby. I just wanted to be alone, to let my mind drift with the soothing choir of crickets and frogs, synching my breath to their punctual chirps. But I was disrupted by the noise—ceaseless, meaningless, disquieting noise.

I stumbled upon a busker stationed in the midst of an intersection, his guitar case open at his feet with only a few stray coins decorating the lining. Was this the life I had forced onto Paolo? The man had a lovely singing voice, and his strums were fluid, but he couldn't garner the attention of the throbbing crowds. Perhaps New Yorkers were too adept at tuning the world out, and no man, not even Paolo, could break through their trances. He had mentioned the fallacy of making it big in a city—it wasn't a sure thing just because you set up shop in the middle of a tourist hub or booked a gig with a local bar. You were one of millions fighting for attention, and even then, attention was no longer a currency you could survive on.

Feeling guilty, I strolled over to a park bench and took out my phone. I dialled without looking at the buttons, and suddenly Stacey was on the other end. She always knew what to do. Though we were the same age, her advice was sage and sound. It was as though she harbored the memories of every generation before her and was able to parse through their mistakes, their adventures, and their worries in order to ground me with her words. Sometimes, I went to her instead of my mother, trusting that Stacey would have an answer no one else could think of and that her wisdom would be right. I always lauded her for her keen senses, but she rebuffed the praise—she didn't aim to be the girl who could claim *I told you so*, she was merely doing the best she could to actually help her loved ones.

"There she is," Stacey chimed. I could hear the grin in her voice. "My city girl."

"Hah, not quite," I replied. My body went into shock at the idea of a new identifier for me—was I really changing that quickly?

"Come on, I bet you're having so much fun. And if you're not, you deserve to let loose for a while. You know, after everything you've been through."

"Yeah..." I didn't want to dwell on that. I couldn't. If I succumbed to my grief now, I wouldn't be able to claw my way back out. I had to keep pushing ahead—to create a life for myself that would have made my mother proud. "It's hard when there's this guy."

"Who?" Her enthusiasm was that of a girl at brunch about to receive juicy gossip, and my heart panged at the idea of turning Paolo into an anecdote.

"He's this guy. He, uh, sings at my dad's old place. Belmont's. And he's trying to stop me from selling it."

"Does he have stock in it?"

"No! No... and that's the crazy thing. He just likes to sing there sometimes, even if the crowd doesn't respond to him, and he's acting as though I'm ripping his livelihood away. He's frustrating, combative, and constantly going out of his way to tank my meetings. I don't know what his problem with me is, considering he hardly even knows me."

"Oh, I thought this was going to be a love story."

"I mean, he is very handsome. And..." I blushed at the idea of admitting our affair. "Well, we've had sex a few times."

She laughed. "So this *is* a love story."

"Absolutely not. He hates my guts, and he told me to my face. I'm really not sure why he won't stop bothering me and what I did to deserve it."

"He doesn't want you to sell the bar."

"Correct."

"Maybe you shouldn't."

I fought back the urge to hang up. Stacey wasn't trying to hurt me with her suggestion, and I couldn't continue my streak of turbulence. I was leaving people in my wake, and I didn't feel good about that, even if some of them made it difficult to behave otherwise. "What do you mean?" I asked, cautious to keep my voice steady.

"Okay, so this guy is a little strange. But I think his heart is in the right place, even if neither of you realize it. Like, why shouldn't you run the bar?"

"He didn't tell me to do that. I think he offered that up as a deal once just to placate me," I corrected.

"That doesn't make him wrong, though, and that doesn't mean you shouldn't do it."

"But I don't want to. Why does nobody care about that pretty crucial detail?"

"So you're just gonna come back to Virginia and keep waiting tables? And then what?"

"Then, that's it. That's all. I have the quiet life I've been carefully cultivating for years."

"You have nothing to come back to."

"I have you, don't I?"

"Abby, I don't want to be here forever," she said with a sigh. "I'm stuck, but I'm trying to find my way out. You can't live your life for other people, especially when they're not gonna do the same for you. I love you, don't get me wrong, but I can't stand in place because of that. We'll be friends no matter where we go or who we are. I believe that wholeheartedly, but you can't stunt your growth out of fear of losing me."

I could feel the tears welling up again, her words ringing in my ears like the bells of truth. I didn't want to believe it, but then, is anyone ever ready to have their lives changed and uprooted? I stalled it for as long as I could, but I was about to start experiencing the growing pains of adulthood I thought I had evaded. People were moving away, spreading out across the country, and altering the plans we thought had been set in stone.

"I don't want to be alone, Stacey. I don't have parents, I don't have any other friends—"

"But you'll make new ones, sweetheart! You already have a boy falling all over you. Think of all the other people you'll meet in a place like New York. You're one of the lucky ones, Abby, even if you can't see that just yet. You're too big for Virginia now. It's an easy place and an easy life that'll bore you in a few years. Don't settle."

"I'm scared," I replied in a hushed voice, the cries I was struggling to choke down caught in my throat. I loved my community—I didn't like the implication that I was above them just because my daddy owned a bar and that I had to flee them at any opportunity that presented itself. But I couldn't deny the stagnation I had forced myself into. In my efforts to defy my father, to right his wrongs, I drove my heels into a place I wasn't sure about anymore. Stacey had put into words what only drifted in my subconscious as a series of inexplicable emotions.

"I know. I am, too. But we'll visit each other. We'll make it work."

"Are you sure?"

"Positive."

***

I found myself back at Belmont's, walking through the crowd with my arms timidly clinging to my sides, swallowing the bile in my esophagus as I prepared to enter the backroom. I couldn't make a decision without looking at the finances—I may not have been a businesswoman, but I could pour over the numbers enough to get the gist of what went on behind closed doors. I didn't want the staff to defy me, though, to regard me as the traitor Paolo had surely told them I was. I clung to the keys in my right hand as if the proof of my ownership would sway them in a last-ditch effort to seize control. I hated being in a battle over something I still didn't fully understand— the bar, my feelings toward it, my relationships with these people. What did I owe them, and what did they owe me? Was that even worth considering at all?

But as I pushed my way through the throngs of people, a familiar grasp landed on my shoulder. A cold shiver went through my nervous system, and I loathed how my reaction had changed to his touch. I didn't want to be afraid of Paolo, to feel hurt whenever he was in my presence. Despite our bickering, I didn't detest him the way he claimed to hate me. I still hadn't shaken off what he'd said the other night, and I wasn't confident I could stop the waterworks should he barrage me with another round of insults.

However, "I'm sorry" was the first phrase that fell off his curled lips. And I caved. I melted. Was I a fool to keep engaging in this toxic relationship? I let him pull me into the kitchen and huddle me against the fridge, out of the way of the cooks but with enough noise to cover our voices over the working staff.

"I've been such a jerk," he continued, "I'm stressed, upset with myself and my choices, and now I'm taking it out on you. I know saving Belmont's won't change my life. I gotta get off my ass and do something about it."

"I've been an asshole, too," I admitted.

"Your parents just died," he replied, his voice quiet as he placed a palm on my shoulder.

"That's not an excuse."

"It sure as hell is."

"Well..." I looked around at the men and women moving about the kitchen. They had smiles on their faces as they chatted over the deep fryers, passed plates to each other, and wiped down their workstations. I saw signs of people who had forged friendships, who had invested time into this building for one reason or another. I wanted to tell Paolo I was considering running Belmont's, but I didn't want to get his hopes up. Not again.

"Listen, I'm taking your advice and revamping my music. It's just not working, and I'm sorry that I snapped at you for pointing that out."

"It's okay, Paolo. We all get touchy about the things we care about."

"Yeah, but that's not an excuse." He winked at me as though we had just created an inside joke of our own. A shared sentiment to return to whenever we found ourselves back in this position—fraught and angry, but trying to make amends.

"Are you making an album?" I asked.

"I don't know," he sighed, taking his hand off my shoulder and running it through his hair.

"Why not?"

He shrugged. "It's a lot of money that I don't have, and nobody's interested in taking another chance on me. Not after my last failure."

"But you need to make an album. How else are you supposed to call yourself a musician?"

"I know... I know..."

Then the idea came to me. "I'll cut you a deal."

"Yeah? You wanna produce my stuff?" His expression was obviously playful, but perhaps part of him was hoping I had a secret recording studio up my sleeve.

"No, but I'll give you the motivation."

"I think sex might be counterproductive to working—"

"Stop. No, I meant that you clearly have an issue with execution. You get in your head, convince yourself of one thing or another, and suddenly, time has passed, and you've neither written anything nor promoted your work. Am I wrong?"

"No, not at all, actually."

"Alright, so what you need is a kick in the ass, and I'll wager running Belmont's in exchange for a completed album."

"What?"

"Yeah. I'll hold off on selling the bar, but only until the end of the month. If, and only if, you have a fully recorded and ready-to-go album by then, will I keep Belmont's open and manage it myself."

"You don't—you don't wanna be here, Abby..."

"I might. And maybe what I need to make that decision is a little motivation. We can help each other, yeah?"

He forcefully grabbed my hand and stiffened my arm. He shook our enclosed palms and smiled as my word became law. "It's a deal," he replied.

Chapter 12:

Paolo

Potential stood before me. Who knew it was going to be dressed up in luscious hair, soft lips, and flushed cheeks? She put many offers on my table, all of which I'd be a fool not to lap up. There was an album, one that would hopefully pivot my stale life and career, propelling me into my next chapter. There was a partnership at Belmont's, where I'd surely worm my way into working alongside her when she took over the business. There was love, the kind that burned bright and never faded. Even if we parted ways somewhere down the line, the memory of our relationship would linger, following us to new people, new homes, and new commitments. We'd compare every romantic encounter to our chemistry, measuring the connection based on an impossible standard. We'd have to knowingly settle, wondering what could have been and making peace with never finding out. That was still preferable to never having been in her life at all, to letting her walk out of that kitchen with crushed dreams and false promises. Why she was making a bet with me, I wasn't certain, but that didn't mean I should scrutinize it until she retracted her statement.

But I was scared. I didn't know why she placed so much faith in me and so erroneously. It wasn't like she could trust me, and I certainly didn't have a track record worth remembering. To her, I should have been a wasted investment, a man who was certainly doomed to fail. To put her own career on the line, as if I was worth the gamble, was perplexing. Madness or romantic compulsion, it didn't make much of a difference. She was putting her fate in my hands, and I couldn't disappoint her. I was done disappointing myself, too.

She didn't know it, but I had to promise myself to stay away from her if only to force myself to keep my head down. It wasn't that she was an irksome distraction, but that with so much riding on me, I couldn't look away from the prize, not even for a second. I scoured the internet for up-and-coming producers who were desperate for clients and bartered with them until I could secure equipment and recording spaces. I created social media accounts purely for my work, and I used every embarrassing hashtag in my captions to boost my visibility. I hunkered down—no drinking, no partying, and only setting foot in Belmont's to perform. Which wound up being every night.

It was difficult to avoid Abigail in those moments: I saw her cheering me on from the sidelines, cupping her hands around her mouth to radiate her pride after every song. We'd have brief conversations once I got off stage, and I could feel her struggling to keep me in her orbit. Her fingers would cling to my shirt, trying to pull me in close, but I'd tug myself away. It was necessary, and she'd understand when I finally told her, when I completed my end of the bargain. Because that was another issue: I was falling behind.

Even with my efforts, constructing a song entirely from scratch, using my own talents to accomplish the task, was time-consuming. I was practically sleeping in the studio—which was makeshift, with sound-proofing purchased from Amazon lining the walls of my producer's closet and equipment salvaged from thrift stores to be filtered through GarageBand. Steven was just as dedicated to my craft as I was, offering me homemade meals between sessions and placing as many phone calls as he could to venues in search of a new home for me. It wasn't enough to keep lighting up the same spot.

The attitude did change at Belmont's, though, and the crowds were packing the place, all of whom were there to see me. Johnny was acting as security, counting the patrons who filed in and cutting them off when the place was bursting at the seams. He ran out of draft beers a few times, citing an inability to keep up with the sudden demand, and Abigail was in the backroom, flooding the books with orders she was nervous to place. She hadn't been around long enough to accurately determine whether or not this was a fluke and didn't want to throw money down the drain, especially if she was going to hand it off in a few short weeks. Because my due date was creeping up quickly, and I still only had half an album to my name.

Part of me was frustrated that she was clinging so tightly to the rules of the bet. I wanted to pull her aside, to convince her to commit to the reigns of Belmont's and make decisions that would keep them afloat forever, but I couldn't interfere. She wasn't counting down the days, sending me messages that felt like thinly veiled threats. She wasn't haggling me behind the scenes, pestering me about the lack of new material. She obviously knew how much I'd done, for I sang the same songs over and over again, only tweaking the riffs or the melodies, trying to figure out what played best. But no, she had backed off, giving me the space I needed to follow through on my tasks. I couldn't hound her, then, even if I felt it was the right choice.

It was the night before the album was due, and I still had yet to complete it. I stood in the office, peeping through the window in the door to gaze out at the crowd. Abigail had been continually popping her head in and out, informing me of the obscene crowd that had gathered. They were turning people away, which Abigail feared would come back to haunt them, but she couldn't make the space for them.

I observed her desk, which she had quickly taken over with coffee rings, old files dusted off and sorted through, and pictures of her parents pinned to a corkboard. She purchased binders and folders, cabinets and computers, and when I asked what she intended to do with everything should I fumble, she merely shrugged and said she'd tack it to the price of the bar. What were another few hundred dollars when people were already prepared to spend millions? At that point, the money weighed as much as pennies. I looked at her penmanship, her name signed on orders and checks, and I wondered why she had gambled something she obviously wanted. She was good at it, too, which had been a surprise. She managed to clear up her father's missteps and small debts, all without asking for help from Johnny or hiring new staff. It was innate—a part of her brain, of her functioning, that all clicked into place once she sat in that office chair and went to work.

I was letting her down, wasn't I? It couldn't be true, I had worked so tirelessly to make that true, and yet it was the final hour, and there I was, holed up in her office, spinning stories of songs I was going to perform tonight that would magically make this all happen for her. But there was nothing new. Nothing she hadn't heard before, save for something that had yet to be recorded. Something I'd had up my sleeve since that night I wrote about her but was too scared to put out into the world. It didn't align with my current project, but maybe it would prop my lie up long enough that Abigail wouldn't realize I had failed her once again.

There was a knock at the door, and suddenly, she was in the cramped room with me, breathing into my neck with an eager beam on her face. "An album release party would make us a killing," she said.

"Oh yeah?" I replied. "Who for?" It was obnoxious to play dumb, but I didn't have a choice. I couldn't reveal my hand.

"You! Don't be silly." She hurried over to the desk, and flipped through the dense layers of pages, looking for something she'd never tell me what it was. "I can get started on the list tonight. All the supplies we'll need. Maybe we can find a beer that relates to your music, like the name of your album, or your name, period. Or maybe we can have labels specially made. You should ask your producer; see what he says. Maybe he has connections. Oh, who am I kidding, he definitely has connections. What's his name again?"

"Steven," I gulped.

"Steven. Exactly. Is he here tonight?"

"No. Why—why would he be?"

"Because it's the big night!" She grabbed onto my shoulders and gently shook me like a doll. I knew she was trying to bolster me, to instill some excitement in me, but it only filled me with dread.

"Not yet."

"Don't be modest, Paolo."

"I'm—I'm..." I sighed, "you're right."

She stepped closer to me, the manic energy radiating off her, finally subduing me as she placed a hand on my face and looked deeply into my eyes. The warmth of her complexion soured me, reminding me of the goodness she deserved and that I was incapable of giving to her. "Who would've thought we'd be here?" she asked with a smile.

I tried to respond—I blinked, I stammered, I leaned into her touch, but my words were gone. I was drained.

"You know, when you first told me to keep Belmont's, I thought you were crazy. Like, had some weird vendetta, out to get me, strange shit," she continued.

"How romantic," I laughed.

"Exactly, not romantic. But you came into my life for a reason, I think. Whether you knew it or not. And I know this seems dramatic and overly sentimental for what we're doing, but I don't know. I have a really good feeling about all of it. I have a good feeling about New York now. About my life. I have a good feeling about you. It took us a while to see eye to eye, but now that we're there, it's... it's right."

All I could do was nod. My face dropped, and so did her hand. Her brows furrowed as she watched my face, looking for any indication of recognition, or love, or something like it. I couldn't fake it, and she took that to heart, stumbling away from me with the composure of a teenager being rejected at the school dance. She combed her hair with her fingers and chuckled a little out of embarrassment.

"I'll see you out there," she said, straightening out her clothes.

I gave her another nonverbal answer.

Luckily, the crowd throbbed around me, sucking me into their vortex as I pushed through them to the stage. They absorbed me, and for a moment, I forgot what was at stake. What I was doing. I was Paolo, again, the singer. The writer. The man they had come here to see. Nothing but the next hour was important—their reactions were my priority, and nothing was going to distract me from my purpose.

As I strummed my guitar, I found myself transported back to my bedroom. The feelings, the passion, the clarity. My fingers effortlessly floated across the neck, pressing and plucking, echoing beautiful chords that brought her face into view. Her name enveloped me. So did her love. I had no choice but to sing about her. Though I had already resolved to pad out my set with the song, hidden away for so long, it was another thing to actually be touting it out. To let the words blare through a microphone. But it was happening, and just as Abigail said, it felt right. I was meant to sing this song the same way she was meant to stumble into my life. We had serendipitously intertwined our desires and come away with something peculiar and special. We would never be able to replicate this again, perhaps not even within our own relationship, and so we had to savor it. This night, this moment. A love like ours was tough to come by.

Chapter 13:

Abigail

It was about me. He sang it like a lullaby, like a demure secret. He sang it with a conviction he never showed me. Mere minutes ago, we were in my office. I was reaching out to him, and he was pulling away—sinking deeper into the solitude I was forced to grow accustomed to, that distant partnership he had carefully cultivated in an effort to do what? I was not certain. My feet were carrying my body out the door, an innate instinct I knew not to question. This was it. This was my entire world finally collapsing on me. Death, love, hopelessness—it was all there, swimming in the currents of my bloodstream and pooling in my extremities. I was on fire.

I heard the crowd roaring inside as Paolo finished his set. I heard the scraping of stools and chairs on the dingy floors as people stood to applaud him. He was basking in the glory of their praise and adoration and was surely gearing up to weaponize it against me. This is what I wanted, right? He would throw it in my face like a sword and laugh as the wound expanded across my skull. Once again, I had been fooled, used as fodder for his music and hosting his performances without batting an eye. He didn't think of me kindly—I was his muse, but our relationship was all fantasy for the masses. It was a mockery.

"Abigail!" he called out to me, but I was already tearing down the street, eyeing the red light of the road crossing before me like a doomed emblem. If I ran, I'd end up waiting at the corner, giving Paolo enough time to catch up to me, but if I stalled or changed routes, I'd probably wind up cornered by him, anyway. I was trapped.

"Leave me alone!" I hollered back, continuing my streak of operating on gut feelings. No matter how childish and insecure, I was going to do it.

"What's wrong *now*?" he shouted back.

"Everything!"

"For crying out loud..."

That did it for me. I had waited like a sitting duck in New York for the last month, tepidly fashioning Belmont's into an establishment I could actually take pride in while my credit card was on hold with a hotel a few blocks away. I was sinking further into potential debt as my inability to make a decision prevented me from finding roots in an apartment, foolishly believing that if I just held out a little longer, Paolo and I would eventually work something out together. *Together.* I wasn't mad at him, I was mad at myself—I had all these expectations I didn't vocalize and here they were, unraveling before me like a cheap spool of thread.

"Your song is a lie!" I yelled, spinning around to confront him.

"What do you mean?"

"You don't love me, Paolo. And yet you get on stage, and you tell these people, some of whom know me, that I am beautiful and wonderful, and worth the world, and blah blah blah... but when we're alone, you just... you don't like me, I know that. You told me as much, and I shouldn't have bought your bullshit when you tried to apologize. Because all you see me as is a character in your story. Someone to manipulate, gaslight, and fuck. If you felt the way you described in that song, we would have been together by now. I wouldn't be fucking homeless in New York holding out hope for you."

"I'm so confused, Abigail," he said, "I've been working on my album for the last month, like you told me to! This was all your idea, and I'm supposed to apologize for listening? You've been complaining about my behavior, and so I fixed it, but now it's a problem because I'm not the man you thought I was or wanted me to be. And as for *love*—"

"I know you don't love me," I replied solemnly, the state of the rejection finally catching up to me.

"That's not true."

I couldn't bear to see the glint of deception in his eyes, and so I kept my gaze trained on the pavement. "You're right. I thought I was going to get some new and improved version of you. Someone who opened up to me like he clearly wanted to all those nights before. Like, you pursued me when we were at each other's throats, and now, as we've been spending time together and getting along, you want nothing to do with me."

"That's *not* true," he repeated, grabbing my hands in a bid to appeal to me. "My song is about you."

"I know."

"Then you know that I love you."

"Wrong."

"How can you tell me I'm wrong about how I feel?"

"Because if you were being honest, you wouldn't have a track record of pushing me away. Even earlier this evening... you couldn't wait to get away from me. I came onto you, if only vaguely, and you got freaked out. It stung, alright? Ever since the duet, which you got so mad at me about, it's like the idea of collaborating with me is repulsive to you. Maybe I tried to tell myself that that wasn't true because I loved you, and those emotions weren't going away. I can take responsibility for that. But you led me on just enough to get glances, and lines, and experiences to put in your lyrics. You used me... again."

"I'm sorry if that's the way you feel, but I haven't been doing any of the things you're accusing me of."

"Then what was that in my office?"

"I don't—"

"You don't know. You never know. But what I see is a man who is so terminally afraid of opening up to people and actually being vulnerable that he has shut himself off from the world. That's why you can't figure out what your audience wants. That's why you still live with your parents. It's easier to pretend to be some stoic man living in solitude, perpetually misunderstood than it is to be known by someone. I thought I was finally going to be that person for you, and that was my mistake."

I started walking away again, feeling confident that I had gotten it all off my chest. It hurt coming up, but the relief was overwhelming as I finally made myself heard. Even I had to announce that to myself— that Paolo was holding himself back, and I couldn't stagnate with him.

"I'm not living with my parents because I'm not vulnerable enough, Abigail. That's such a stupid thing to say."

"Whatever!" I replied, my back still facing him. I didn't hear footsteps following, and I knew that I had broken through to him. For better or for worse, he understood what I had said.

"Sorry that I didn't have a bar handed to me, and I actually have to work my ass off to make a living! If it were so easy, of course, I would have moved out! I'm stuck there!"

"Enough with the excuses, Paolo! You are a grown man! Act like one!" I decided to take one last look at him to gauge his emotions through his rugged countenance. What I saw was the resentment of a teenage boy. "Momma told me to chase after you right before she died. That you might be the one or something. I followed her advice for long enough, but she's not here anymore, and I gotta live for me."

"Good to know I was your pity date. Now, I won't feel bad about never seeing you again."

We stood there, bitterness in the air as we remained frozen in place. I had continued my streak of allowing the truth to fall off my tongue without thinking it through, but perhaps I had taken it too far. I wasn't wrong, but I didn't feel good about it either. Momma didn't want me to use her words against people—she was just trying to give her daughter permission to fall in love. Something I had never done before. Something I had always wanted. Something I imagined would torment me, and I was right. I couldn't explain the way my entire body crashed in on itself, folding and melting and collapsing like a pile of sticks someone had knocked over. I wasn't sure how I'd ever be able to breathe again.

This was a moment I'd be thinking about for the rest of my life.

***

When I got back to the hotel, my card key wasn't working. I tried the handle a million times like a moron before I finally gave up the fight and slumped down to the concierge's desk. I swore he was waiting for me: He had a smug smile on his face, and my information was pulled up on his computer within seconds. This was a planned attack.

"Your card declined," he informed me with a snotty tone.

"That's not possible," I retorted, refusing to believe I had succumbed to another horrid fate. I just wanted to be on my bed, the one that had finally started to morph into my body shape, wear a disappointingly stiff robe, and watch TV until I forgot where I was.

"It is." I could hear the dryness of his mouth as his lips moved and curved over his overly white teeth.

"Check again."

"Why don't *you* check again, Miss Belmont?"

"I know how much money I have on that card."

"Do you?"

"I'm not in the mood for these games," I warned, as if I was someone to be reckoned with. Perhaps I could pretend to be important, like a Senator's daughter or a C-list celebrity quickly climbing the social ladder.

"And I only serve guests who pay." There seemed to be a thrill in denying me, a pleasure he derived from the misery of the revelation.

"I have paid. I do pay."

"Come back when you can afford your stay."

"I am staying here already. You people have all my shit. I mean, where is all my luggage anyway? Is it being held for ransom?"

But then I was on my ass in front of the hotel, sitting on my suitcase as I waited for help to arrive. I hoped other patrons would notice my predicament, take pity on me, and invite me into their room. I eyed the doorman like he was a knight in shining armor—he had the ability to save me from my terrible luck. He avoided me with an intensity that I couldn't deny, even if he never vocalized it. I wanted to shout curse words at him, but I knew he was only doing his job. If the concierge had the power to make my life hell, I figured the doormen were just as vulnerable to the reign of terror.

Reluctantly, I got out my phone and swiped through my contacts, of which there were only four: my mother, the lawyer, Stacey, and Paolo. The tears were back as I looked at my list, and realized I had ostracized the only person in this city who could care about me. It would have been cruel of me to reach out, to demand comfort and solace in the same breath that I called him a coward. I hurt his feelings and then went back for seconds as if he was incidental to me the way I accused him of treating me.

Did I have any other choice, though? I had nothing to my name—no money, no shelter, no family—and New York wasn't a place I was comfortable loitering around at night. I needed a ride to Belmont's, at the very least. Just somewhere to rest my head while I poured through the finances I had apparently tanked. I needed one last nudge, and then I'd leave him alone forever. I knew that's what he wanted.

I bit my tongue as I dialled his number and was shocked when he picked up on the first ring.

Chapter 14:

Paolo

I attempted to dull the humming in my ears as I picked up the phone, and Abigail's weepy voice came through the speaker. It was hazy and jagged; the electronic particles that pulled it apart and reassembled it had butchered the sweetness of her tone. It was her, but it also wasn't. She was somewhere far away, as distant as she claimed me to be, and the idea of her departure made me melancholic. I wanted to be angry with her, to continue the feud we had cultivated over the last month, but as I had come to realize, I was weak. Softened by time and emotion, I allowed Abigail to plead her case, knowing I was always going to bend to her wishes.

"Can you pick me up?" she asked, a slight croak emanating from her vowels.

"Where?" I sighed, still standing outside of Belmont's with my free hand wedged deep into my pocket. The bouncer stared at me, having witnessed our fight, but he offered no words of advice.

"The hotel. They kicked me out."

"What did you do?" The question came out like an accusation, and I regretted it swiftly.

"Nothing, it's just my... my credit card bounced. I'm all maxed out."

"Sunk it into the bar." Sunk it into me. She still hadn't been told the album wasn't finished, though I'm sure she gathered that on her way out.

"Yeah," she agreed.

"I'll be there soon."

"Really?"

"Of course. Because I want to be with you, Abigail."

"Even after everything I said?"

"Especially after that. You're right. I haven't been honest with you, myself, or anyone."

"Okay."

I didn't know what to make of that. But I didn't have time to mull it over, pick it apart, and draw a conclusion that would inevitably be stricken down again. I wasn't the best at keeping a story straight, and Abigail had an impeccable radar for my bullshit. So I sprinted home, the car keys jingling in my pocket as a reminder of what was on the line. The girl I loved was stranded in New York, her entire world at her feet, and it was up to me to help her. To pull her out of this mess.

"I'm coming," I muttered to myself, "just hold on."

***

Abigail piled into my car, defeated. I waited for her to thank me, to tell me she was sorry, but she stared ahead like a zombie, her lips frozen in a perpetual pout. This wasn't the reaction I had expected. Was I doomed to be the asshole, or was Abigail just as responsible for the dissolution of our relationship?

"You're welcome," I said with the aggravated tone of a mother who had spent the entire day cleaning just for her kids to track mud on the floors.

"Yeah... yeah, thank you." She continued to train her eyes on the bumper of the taxi before us.

"Are you alright?" I asked, my tone levelling.

"Of course I'm not, Paolo. I can't keep doing this. I'm in way over my head, and now that I think about it, I never sat down and just *grieved*. I lost both my parents and kept pushing like it hadn't happened to me.

Like they were across the country, and that's why I wasn't seeing them, but I was working hard so I had something to show them eventually. But they're not here. There's nothing."

"We can figure this out," I offered, but no sign of relief crossed her face.

"There's nothing we can do. My finances are my fault, and whether or not you finish the album is mute. I have to come up with the money."

"But I want to help you."

"That's great, but—"

"But nothing, Abigail. This is me trying to be open. This is me showing up for you the way you asked me to. I'm here, picking you up when I didn't have to. I'm here, telling you I'll puzzle out the finances with you. We'll make sure you're set up for life, not for right now, okay?"

"And that's great," she repeated, "*but* it's not about the big gestures. It's not about claiming you're going to follow through with them, either. It's the day-to-day stuff that counts the most, and we could have had that for the last month, but that's when you decided to pull away."

"I'm sorry. I really mean that, too. I'm sorry. But now you're the one digging your head into the sand and trying to push me out. I'm telling you I'm going to be there for you, and you need to let me live up to that. You need to let me prove my word."

When she looked at me, I felt my breath catch in my throat. That magnificent, angelic face was swarmed by doubt, but she nodded anyway. This was the second chance she took on me, and I couldn't squander it this time.

"I'm taking you home," I declared and peeled out of the hotel driveway.

***

I couldn't sleep. The night swirled all around me, my eyes failing to adjust to the darkness. I squinted at shadows that were sometimes furniture and sometimes dead air, trying to make sense of the living room I had known so well. For some reason, it could never hold its familiarity in the blackness of the night, and I found myself yearning for the comforts of my room. I had put Abigail there as a means of repentance—she wouldn't have to stumble into the eyeline of my parents, nor would she have to contemplate her future with me snoring in her ears. She'd be comfortable and relaxed, a much-needed reprieve from her disaster of a day.

But now I was tossing and turning on the couch, struggling to make the blankets reach all the way to my toes and adjusting the stiff pillows every couple of minutes, never liking the way my face mashed into the textured fabric. A grandfather clock ticked endlessly, the noise was a drone that never attached itself to a physical presence. I was trapped with the phantom metronome.

I heard a door creak open, and I squeezed my eyes shut, assuming it was my mom or dad getting up for a glass of water. I didn't want to explain the situation right now, not at this ungodly hour, and I attempted to stave off the conversation by feigning sleep. However, the cushions by my legs sagged as another human weight descended upon them, and whether I wanted to commit to my ruse or not, the person by my feet was going to remain there until I awoke.

"Paolo," she whispered, and I could immediately recognize Abigail's voice.

My eyes fluttered open, and her outline came into view. The moon illuminated the baby hairs that sprung from her head and the carvings of her shapely body.

"I appreciate you," she continued, resting a hand on my waist.

"You do?" I asked, my voice coarser than I thought it would be.

"Of course. You need the opportunity to try, and I need to give you that. This is step one, and already it's meant a lot to me."

"I just want you to be happy," I replied, my hand finding hers in the darkness.

"I could stand to be more open, too. I feel like I've been blaming you for too much. I'm an adult; I have some control over my life. I can't make that your problem."

"They could be *our* problems. You know, if we were partners."

"What kind of partners?" There was an unmistakable excitement in her voice as her tone went up a few octaves.

"Business. Romantic."

"I like the sound of that."

"I think I love you, Abigail." Even in the dark, I could see her eyes widening and the crest of her teeth flashing from underneath her plump lips.

"You only think?"

"Well, I can't love somebody who hates me. You gotta be nice to me first, on a consistent basis."

She gave a small laugh. "How's this for nice?"

And then she slipped her hand from my waist to my boxers, her grip hovering over my already pulsating member. She leaned down for a kiss, and I met her enthusiastically, exploring the warmth of her mouth with my tongue. We heard a sound emanating from the depths of the apartment and stopped in our tracks, listening for signs of my parents.

"Maybe we shouldn't," she whispered, her lips still moving over mine. She was trailing them down my jaw, my neck, and my chest while her hand worked on my cock.

"It's too late," I replied, "I want you so bad."

She climbed on top of me, careful to limit the noises the cushions made as they groaned under our collective weight. She confidently inserted me, gently riding as she pleasured herself, a hand over her mouth to keep herself from moaning. It was like watching a magnificent show—her pale breasts flounced before me, her thighs shook as her needs became more dire, and the contortions of her face were riveting.

For as erotic as the moment was, it was also different from our previous lovemaking. I felt closer to her, more intimate. I felt passion beyond the physical, and I made sure to show it. Flipping her around, I laid her on my bed of blankets and pillows and forced her eyes to meet mine as I thrust in and out. I leaned into the palm she placed on my cheek, burrowed my skin into hers, and let it meld with her scent. I kissed her as I came, allowing the full heat of her body to envelop me as I peaked. She groaned into my ear, something soft and innocent, something about love and togetherness. I responded by taking her back to my room, tucking her under the covers, and wrapping her in my arms.

I made promises to her in the dark that I wasn't sure she had heard— she was still against my body, her chest expanding and contracting with her serene breaths. I didn't dare ask if she was awake for fear of disturbing her, but I continued to chant my declarations into her forehead. I imagined the vibrations of my voice would reach her in her slumber, and she'd register the sentiment in her subconscious. I told her that I would finish my album, that I would dedicate each song to her, and etch the lyrics into the bathroom stalls at Belmont's. I told her that I would finally move out, that I'd been looking at places for a while, and they were within my reach; I was just too scared to take the plunge. I hadn't been on my own for a long time, and I wasn't used to the idea of operating without a safety net. But that was perhaps the reason why my music had never taken off—I didn't feel the need to work my ass off, promote my work, and tour it beyond New York's concrete empire. I knew my parents would be waiting for me when the dust settled, and they'd take care of me until I was back on my feet again or if I never returned to music at all. I had allowed them to bolt me to the ground with training wheels for too long, and it was up to me to set that right.

I apologized for resenting her for wanting to push me to be better and for seeing my potential in ways that nobody else had. I apologized for freaking out when she sang with me—it's not that I didn't like it or understand how fluidly our voices blended together. It's not that I didn't see the potential in our collaboration. It's that she was better than me in every conceivable way, and yet she was choosing me. The idea of having to live up to someone for the rest of my life was daunting, and I wanted to run away from the challenge like a scared little boy. But it wasn't her fault my ego was so easily dismantled, and it wasn't her fault I lashed out at her over my own petty insecurities. I owed her a lot, and the debts wouldn't be worked off for a very long time. That idea, however, no longer frightened me. I wanted to be good for her.

Chapter 15:

Abigail

The sun had barely risen when I left Paolo. I placed a note on his bedside table telling him where to find me and gathered only a few things so he'd be confident I wasn't fleeing. I just needed some fresh air, and New York rarely offered that to me, so I took the train out to Coney Island in hopes that the beach would be empty at this hour and I'd be able to soak in the salt air in solitude. I felt pride as I navigated the myriad of trains that drove me from one burrow to the furthest corners of another as if this was a route I had been travelling my whole life. The girl who emerged from the underground world with her suitcase and a host of naivety was gone, and in her place was a woman who knew what she wanted and where she was going.

I sat in the sand with my knees to my chest and watched as the world came to life around me. Lights flickered on the boardwalk as owners prepared their bars for opening, and the amusement rides tested their gears before patrons arrived in hoards. The waves ebbed at my feet, and for a moment, I missed the beaches of Virginia. I missed the wild horses that trotted through packed sand and the cars full of families that left tire tracks in the mud. I missed making friends with my neighbors sitting beside me under their umbrellas, and I missed the slow pace of a day that was dedicated only to leisure. New York never calmed down. There was only every *go go go*.

As if to solidify my perception of the city, I received a text message alert from the buyer that their offer expired tonight. How were they awake at such an hour? Couldn't I be alone for just two minutes? The troubles of my world pressed against me again like a tide that threatened to swallow me and hold me under. Paolo hadn't finished his album, but was I going to let a bet determine my life? I had forged it because I was scared to make a decision for myself—I wanted fate and the powers that be to make it for me, and they had spoken, had they not? I was to sell the bar because of Paolo. But the idea of following that instruction was terrifying—not because I didn't think I could litigate such a deal, but because I felt I was giving something up, something better. I was taking the easy way through life, and I didn't want to be that person anymore.

I sat on the beach for hours, ignoring the rest of my incoming calls as I mulled over my decision. Regardless of how much energy I expended on my options, none of them stuck out to me. I failed to gravitate toward an answer. I moved from bar to bar, ordering fresh clams and beer. I ate hot dogs and went on the Wonder Wheel, looking out at the city and hoping it would whisper back to me. That it would tell me what to do. I spent so much time at Coney Island that the sun began to dip below the horizon, and I resolved to trek back to Belmont's. Avoiding the issue at hand wasn't going to make it go away—Paolo deserved resolution just as much as the buyer.

It was a somber affair as I pushed through the doors at Belmont's—the bartenders were taking their posts, and the bouncers were checking their gear. Paolo was already on stage, tuning his guitars and playing with the amps until the sound was just right. It had only taken him a month, but he had finally gotten into the habit of showing up early and running through his checklists rather than waiting for a crowd to form and holding them hostage to his menial tasks. I hated that opting to sell the bar felt like a punishment. I didn't want to communicate the notion of failure and misery just because he couldn't meet my arbitrary deadline. Neither could I. We were both paralyzed by what could have been, by our own inaction and lack of direction. We were aimless wanderers, and we should have spent the last month rubbing our heads together to craft magical ideas rather than working in isolation, hoping for a better end result.

As I stared at Paolo, he waved me over to the stage, and I hesitated. Could he see it on my face? The confusion and desperation? What was going to become of my things, which I left in his room and now realized may cause more trouble down the line should I choose to sell the place? He wouldn't spurn me, not after everything we'd been through. I had to put some faith in him, to give him the benefit of the doubt. And as I made my tormented walk over to him, I felt like the clouds were parting.

"You sing tonight," he decried, holding his wingspan out to me as if to curl me into his long embrace.

"What?" I asked, forgetting about my previous troubles.

"You heard me. *You* sing tonight. The people wanna hear you."

"But, Paolo... it was fun that one time. I can't make a career out of it, though."

"Oh, don't take it so seriously, Abigail. I saw the way you were on stage the other night. You like it. This whole bar has been about me—what I want, how I need to be seen—but you're the owner now. You need to tell the world who you are and what you have to say."

"What if I don't know what that is?"

He chuckled warmly. "Cut the bullshit, alright?" He grabbed my hands, craning his neck so his face could meet mine. "You are the most confident, charismatic, intelligent woman I have ever met. You figure shit out, even if you don't realize you're doing it. It's your nature to solve problems and make people better. You lifted me up for the last month, and now it's my job to make you see that as a *thank you*. Besides, you'll have me up there with you, playing you along. You're not alone anymore."

So I sat there with him—he strummed the guitar, and I sang all the notes that came to my heart. I didn't put too much thought into it; just recalled what I could of Paolo's work and started adding my own flair to it. An hour had gone by before I noticed how packed the bar was, each person swarming the stage like we were the next big act. They watched in awe as if this would be a story they told their grandchildren about. Maybe it felt that way to me, anyway. Like I was in a dream, the highest anyone had ever been, and nothing could send me crashing back to earth.

A love like ours,

Don't come around too often.

I resolved to keep the bar and continue running it as the manager. Once our performance was over, I sent a swift text to the buyer, who hadn't bothered to show up—tells you how much their heart was in it—and reached out to my lawyer about acquiring Belmont's formally. Paolo was engaged in a heated conversation with someone he would later tell me was his former manager, who informed him that his label wanted him back. I was not a part of their bargain, so Paolo didn't hesitate to turn them down. He didn't want to be tied down to another contract, anyway. Steven was helping him along just fine, and his album was almost finished. With all the attention we'd managed to bring, he was sure to see a spike in his sales and keep a level of the profit his previous company wouldn't have allowed.

We were flourishing, and it all happened in one night. That nagging, irritating sect of my brain warned me to keep my expectations at bay, but I was tired of listening to it. I was tired of running away. Paolo and I sat at the bar, having a conversation with Johnny and laughing about nothing. For once, I wasn't discussing the tragedies of my present. I wasn't embroiled in the latest stressor in my life. I was talking like the world was ending—animated, silly, and hopeful. I was becoming the person I had always wanted to be in real-time, with Paolo's reassuring hand placed gently on my thigh. We didn't need concrete plans for me to know he'd be leaving his parents' soon, and we'd be scouring the city for a place of our own. Everything that ailed us was temporary, as it always was in life—the bad couldn't keep us down for long. We were on our way up.

A love like ours,

Is touching my heart,

All the time.